BREXIT XXL

A Novel by

Vincent Pluchet

Translated by Margaret Morrison

First published in Great Britain as a softback original in 2018

Copyright © Vincent Pluchet

The moral right of this author has been asserted.

All characters and events in this publication, other than those clearly in the public domain, are fictitious and any resemblance to real persons, living or dead, is purely coincidental.

All rights reserved.

No part of this publication may be reproduced, stored in a retrieval system, or transmitted, in any form or by any means, without the prior permission in writing of the publisher, nor be otherwise circulated in any form of binding or cover other than that in which it is published and without a similar condition including this condition being imposed on the subsequent purchaser.

Typeset in Dante MT Std and Eurostile

Editing, design, typesetting and publishing by UK Book Publishing

www.ukbookpublishing.com

ISBN: 978-1-912183-62-3

Author Bio

An alumni of the London School of Economics and the French École Polytechnique, Vincent Pluchet has a passion for historical and political topics. He works as a consultant in Finance and Strategy in the Middle East, where he has been based since 2004. He was a CFO with a large financial institution for more than fifteen years. He is married with one daughter.

brexitxxl.com

Contents

A pudding with a bitter taste	1
Debate in the British House of Commons	4
Brexit XXL	11
Monsieur Marquet has a problem	15
Sovereignty	20
A Serious Alert	25
The BBC Interviews	28
Meeting between Tracy Meller and Philip Denniel	35
The HGB Bank	39
Tracy Meller discovers the collapse of Construct	46
Chequers	50
The crisis of February 2022	63
The crisis spreads	76
The Democratic Alliance	84
Demonstrations	91
Guy Wick takes action	97
Janet Gradens	106
Campaign Strategies	111
A turbulent summer	117
The Scottish Question	128
More meetings at Chequers	134
Guy Wick's campaign	145
September Divisions	152
Change of direction	162
The new Europe	171
The May 2023 campaign	179
A last weekend in Chequers	185
Referendum	189
Epilogue	191

Addendum:

Brexit from 2016 to 2021	195
Dramatis personæ	203
Thanks and acknowledgements	204

A pudding with a bitter taste

Philip Denniel, the Governor of the Bank of England, invited to lunch at his mother-in-law's house for Christmas Eve of 2021, was slowly chewing a piece of the traditional pudding.

"The pudding does not taste quite like it normally does," he finally observed.

"It's the brandy," replied his mother-in-law. "The French brandy I always bought before is too expensive now. I used a British apple brandy."

Speechless, Denniel stared at his mother-in-law. If even the Christmas pudding was affected by Brexit, what was the country coming to?

Jane Farrow, though, lived in a comfortable house in an affluent part of the city. It was true that this elegant seventy-six-year-old lady had always been cautious with money, especially since her husband's death. But this level of austerity was unprecedented.

The elderly lady excused herself to pop down to the ground floor. Denniel finished his pudding with little enthusiasm, alone in the large dining room with floral wallpaper. His wife and their two daughters, keen to do some last-minute shopping, had made good their escape before pudding was served. Big Ben, or rather the miniature replica on the mantelpiece, chimed two o'clock. The Governor, sunk in his thoughts, barely heard it. So this is what it had come to. The mother-in-law of the Governor of the Bank of England, and probably all the mothers-in-law across the country, were too hard up to buy imported ingredients for their puddings.

"Would you like some more pudding?"

Denniel was roused from his brief distraction by the return of his hostess. He declined politely, got up from the table, and went through into the first floor sitting room next to the dining room. He liked thinking in this room, which was lined with beautiful woodwork and red velvet curtains, well lit by several bay windows, and beautifully decorated with a collection of Chinese ceramics and silver ornaments. Several reproductions of works by Reynolds, Gainsborough and Turner adorned the walls. The Governor had a favourite spot, a leather armchair near the fireplace, where he spent long hours smoking his pipe. But today he was too pre-occupied to sit quietly. Wanting to enjoy the sun that had just come out, he went over to the main window and opened it. In from the quiet London street came December air, chilly, invigorating, freshened by the rain that had fallen that morning.

What could be done to rescue his country from the doldrums? Denniel had been asking himself the same question for two years, without arriving at any conclusion. Unemployment, companies failing, devaluation, inflation... The country had been in recession since 2019. Problems were being heaped upon problems. The Governor was now dreading a still darker prospect, a plunge into an even deeper crisis, which would shake the country to its very foundations.

Looking down the street, he saw a taxi passing too fast, splashing a passer-by. The driver stopped immediately, got out, and could be heard apologising, offering to take the passer-by on to his destination for free. The pedestrian accepted gracefully. "All is not lost," thought Denniel. "We still have a people of great character, able to endure difficulties with phlegm and stoicism."

He decided to go out for a walk, told his mother-in-law on his way through the kitchen and went down to the ground floor. Having put on his coat and a cap, he opened the front door. It was at that moment that he was hit in the face by something congealed and sticky. A piece of Christmas pudding. "Go on, let them eat pudding! This disaster is all your fault!" shouted the man who had thrown it. Denniel wanted to respond, but the projectile thrower had already disappeared. Returning to the house to clean his face, he considered that perhaps the country was not so phlegmatic after all...

The incident did not prevent him from going on to have an uneventful walk. On his return, an hour later, he noticed that his daughters and his wife had not come back. He could not see his mother-in-law either; she had probably gone out as well. He went back to the sitting room, put a log on the fire, lit a pipe, settled down in the leather chair and turned on the television. He decided to watch the last parliamentary debate of the year, which had taken place two days earlier, and which he had not been able to see at the time. It had been widely discussed in the press.

Debate in the British House of Commons

"Honourable and Right Honourable Members, Jeremy Jones, Leader of the Opposition."

The leader of the Labour Party rose, addressing the Speaker and then the Members of Parliament.

"Thank you, Madam Speaker.

"My Honourable Friends know that the country is today in one of the worst situations it has ever known as a result of the decisions taken by the Government over the last five years. The Prime Minister claims to have acted on the will of the people. In fact, she has led the country into a dead end.

"Instead of negotiating decent exit terms with our partners, in the aftermath of the 2016 Referendum, she has, by her intransigence, brought about a unilateral departure from the European Union without a single term favourable to this country. The result, as we all know, has been nothing short of disaster. Our companies and financial institutions have lost direct access to the vast European market. No major trade agreement has emerged to compensate for this loss despite repeated promises by the government. We have seen purchasing power plummet and the relocation of tens of thousands of jobs. Our unemployment rate is huge. The people of this country are suffering.

"The government should have negotiated at the very least an agreement on the Norway model, which would have both respected our autonomy and safeguarded our economy, leaving the country within the European Economic Area. However, blinded by her Little Englander ideology, the Prime Minister has rejected any reasonable path, and since then has persisted in a suicidal isolationist policy."

Jeremy Jones spoke forcefully. The members of his party behind him were visibly pleased with his speech. Everyone was recalling the decision that Tracy Meller, Prime Minister since July 2016, had taken in 2018, to break off the negotiations she had been conducting for more than a year with Brussels to define the conditions under which Britain would leave the European Union following the Brexit Referendum. Meller had believed that these negotiations, which were progressing only with great difficulty and had on several occasions ground to a halt, were heading for an unacceptable deal. Supported by British public opinion, which was angered by what the press called "European arrogance in the negotiations", the Prime Minister had gone to the country in May 2018, on a platform of a unilateral Brexit, resulting in the Conservative party winning one of its most resounding victories. The newly elected Parliament had confirmed the decision and the United Kingdom had left the European Union in March 2019 with no trade agreement with her continental neighbours. The resulting economic impact had been violent and had sent Britain into recession.

Jones continued his speech. Opposite him, Tracy Meller chafed impatiently, surrounded by her Ministers and Conservative MPs.

"In the current situation, there are four major actions that any responsible government should embark on with immediate effect.

"The first is to rejoin the European Economic Area without any preconditions, the only way to reopen markets to our industries.

"The second is to address the state of the country! There is an urgent need to ramp up social programmes and to launch a policy of major public works to encourage household consumption and reboot our economic machine. Instead, this government is suffocating our economy by adding a supply policy which is utterly unfit for purpose to an already desperate situation. Our country is not short on productivity; it is short on consumers, because people simply no longer have the means to buy.

"The third urgent step is to engage in real discussions with the devolved regions, Scotland, Wales and Northern Ireland. While the nation has remained unified so far as a result of the moderation and prudence of the regional authorities, we know that this is no longer sustainable and that there is a real risk of the country breaking apart if we do not change course soon.

"Finally, the fourth measure, which is one for the Prime Minister personally, is to stop dreaming and stop lying to the electorate. Making the country believe that it can regain its past greatness by going it alone, maximizing British competitive advantage, is an illusion. This is not the Britain of the eighteenth and nineteenth centuries. The time when decisions were taken in London is over. Britain represents less than one percent of the world's population. It is only through solid links to the European Union, with countries who are both partners and friends, that our nation can continue to exist, develop, and retain a global influence commensurate with our historic ambitions.

"That is what a responsible government would do. That is, unfortunately, what the Conservative government has been unable to do since 2016. That is why I formally request, given the seriousness of the political and economic situation, that the Prime Minister dissolves Parliament and calls a General Election, so that the British electorate, with full knowledge of the facts, and not relying on false promises like in 2018, can choose their future destiny."

Jeremy Jones, red faced and sweating, sat down amidst prolonged applause from his own party. It was the first time he had called for the dissolution of Parliament. Labour MPs knew that the mood of the electorate had changed dramatically since their great defeat in 2018, due to both the wearing down effect of the economic situation, and demographic changes: more and more young people, in favour of a return to Europe, were reaching voting age and couldn't wait to change the future of their country. A general election would therefore most likely be won by Labour, the only party advocating a return to the European Union. Jones' request was possible because the Fixed-Term Parliament Act of 2011 had been repealed in 2020, so the Prime Minister had regained her customary right to call an early election.

"Honourable and Right Honourable Members, the Prime Minister."

Tracy Meller rose with relief, partly because she was eager to refute Jeremy Jones' arguments, but mainly because her position sitting on the House of Commons benches squashed between her fellow Ministers was decidedly uncomfortable. She always wondered why the architects who designed Parliament, when they rebuilt the building after the fire of 1834, had created such a small Chamber, obliging the Members to squeeze into a few rows, an arrangement which was preserved when the Chamber, destroyed once again during the 1941 blitz, was rebuilt in 1950. Anyone arriving late had to follow the debates standing up, as the Chamber could only hold about two thirds of the Members.

But what government would dare to make major changes to this historic place these days? Certainly not hers, when she had become the champion of immutable British traditions, and certainly not during the Westminster renovations planned for the following years (requiring at some point a temporary relocation of the two Chambers), every detail of the specifications for the work having already been scrutinised exhaustively. Tracy Meller took the floor.

"The Right Honourable gentleman claims we are dreaming – well, it's he who is fast asleep!" (Laughter from the Government benches.) "In his sleep befuddled state he does not seem to recall that not once but twice, in 2016 and in 2018, the voters sent an unmistakable message about the direction they wanted to see the country take. The Right Honourable gentleman seems to believe that these decisions were not valid, and that if we asked the voters to give their opinion yet again, they would express a different one. I would like to remind him that in a democratic country we take voting seriously, and we do not decide to call another election just because we were not happy with the previous result.

"I also note that in the cosy dreams the Leader of the Opposition is enjoying, the State is far richer than in the real world, and it is possible to incur considerable expenditure to revive the economy. I am sorry to have to wake the Right Honourable Gentleman so abruptly but I would like to enquire as to just where the State is to find money that it does not have? In the local authorities under Labour control perhaps?" (More laughter from the Government benches, Tracy Meller's remarks referring to two Labour authorities which had just gone bankrupt, due, of course, to their mismanagement, according to the Conservatives.)

Jeremy Jones could not contain himself.

"It is unacceptable, Madam Speaker, for some people to make the desperate position of local governments in our country a laughing matter."

A clamour of voices rose in the Chamber and the Speaker had to call for order.

Tracy Meller continued, speaking with renewed vigour.

"What is unacceptable is to make the citizens of this country believe that easy options will serve them well. A botched agreement with Europe will not. Nor will unaffordable public spending. This country has often had to make difficult choices, and it is those choices which have made it great.

"The Leader of the Opposition claims that our economic situation is disastrous. That supposes you only look at certain current figures, without seeing the wider trends that reflect the gradual transformation of our nation. The Right Honourable gentleman may not be able to see this, but our country, freed from nit picking control from Brussels, has made sweeping reforms, which would have been impossible to put in place during our membership of the European Union.

"While the twenty-seven European countries, trapped in complex decision-making processes, have not been able to do much more than tweak their policies in the face of the last few years of drastic global change, our government, free of all constraints, has started work on the foundations of the future of our country. For convincing examples, you have only to look at these four sectors:

"Firstly, digital technology: the UK, thanks to devaluation and our tax breaks, has become extremely competitive across all sectors of software and internet services, which are the key industries for this century.

"Secondly, scientific and medical research, another forward thinking area in which our country has always shone, has seen a great leap forward.

"Thirdly, literature, music and art: our production companies and publishers are among the best in the world and have taken advantage of the economic situation to expand.

"Fourthly, education and tourism: we are receiving unprecedented numbers of foreign students and visitors.

"Yes, the last five years have been a difficult, painful transition for many people. But this is now a liberated country that is finally making long-deferred adjustments. We are heading for a future which will see a stronger Britain, with an economy based on our real competitive advantages. That is the plan we have laid out, and this is certainly not the time, in the midst of such fundamental changes, to start calling elections whose sole purpose would be to further the political ambitions of the Leader of the Opposition."

Tracy Meller sat down, amidst applause from the Conservative Party and boos from the Labour benches.

Philip Denniel switched the television off. He had listened to the debate carefully, even though he was very familiar with the usual lines of the main players. He considered there was some merit to the Prime Minister's analysis. However, as he knew the figures better than anyone, he was well aware that the transition period referred to by Meller was far from over. While not strictly speaking lies, her claims only touched on a tiny fraction of the real situation, ignoring whole sectors that had been hit terribly hard by Brexit, like the industrial, agricultural and financial sectors, which had lost hundreds of thousands of jobs. The situation was far more serious than Meller was prepared to say. At the moment, thought the Governor, there were a host of economic threats, the risk of a major crisis was higher than ever, and the country was certainly in for some strong turbulence...

Brexit XXL

Tracy Meller left Downing Street, crossed Whitehall, went down Richmond Terrace, a small alleyway to which she had access, and headed along the banks of the Thames, towards Embankment station. She was an elegant woman in her sixties, always well dressed in classic lines from the best designers. Her hair, which she kept shoulder length and well-coiffed, had once been blonde, and had now been allowed to turn grey which added to her serious air. Medium-height, as careful of her figure as she was of her outfits, she had remained slim. She had been in the habit of walking for exercise for many years and had maintained this habit since she became Prime Minister, walking for an hour, followed by two bodyguards.

Her security detail had originally protested, suggesting alternative routes which were easier to secure, but she had stood her ground, wanting to be able to stroll freely around London, her beautiful city. The only concession the protection team had obtained was that she changed her itinerary each time and warned them in advance so that they could carry out a reconnaissance of the route.

Today she was particularly in need of her walk. She had left Parliament with a headache after the stormy proceedings. She had been supported by her party, but she was well aware that it was all a façade. The reality was that her popularity was in freefall, both in the country and within her own camp, and several of her ministers were just waiting for an opportunity to stab her in the back and take her place. The only thing that held them back was that they wanted her to carry on being the public target for the unpopularity caused by the economic situation, while they waited for an upturn that would be their opportunity to act.

She listened to the cries of the seagulls, took a deep breath, and walked on quietly. She had chosen this route, rather than a walk in St James's Park, which she was also fond of, to see the busy city. Watching the boats on the Thames, hearing the sounds of trains and Tubes, seeing people leaving their offices, all this bustle reassured her, gave her hope for the country.

She took a moment to lean on the parapet of the Embankment and look at the river. Opposite her, London Eye, the big wheel, was turning constantly. The lights in the buildings were starting to come on. It was surprisingly good weather for one of the last days of December; the sky was dotted with white clouds, and the temperature remained mild for the season, despite a chilly breeze.

She pulled her coat tighter around her, and resumed her walk, greeting passers-by, who were always pleasant when she met them during her walks. She had never had children, which was one of the sorrows of her life, and could not help feeling a pang every time she saw a family. She often posed for photos with children. In those moments she would have abandoned her brilliant career, all the honours, for the simple pleasure of holding her own little blond-haired child in her arms. She supposed she had thrown herself into politics to forget, and had devoted her life to it, being first a Mayor, then an MP, and then a Minister. She was not chasing fame, though, just trying to serve her country.

When her predecessor had announced that he was resigning, five years previously, she had stood for election within her party. She had certainly not been indifferent to the possibility of becoming Prime Minister, the summit of any political ambition in Britain. But she had mainly stood out of a sense of duty, because she believed she was one of the few to be able to lead the nation in difficult times.

Tenacious, hardworking, incorruptible, she was respected by her party and had been elected easily and quickly. However, she was not unaware that many of the influential figures of the party had supported her leadership bid because they did not want to take the leading role themselves for the risky situation ahead.

Her political masterstroke was the May 2018 election, which her party had won with a large majority, and which had reinforced her position. The expression "Brexit XXL" had been invented by one of the tabloids during the campaign. It was their nickname for the idea of a kind of supersized Brexit, with no half measures. The country would take its destiny into its own hands, alone, all the way. All British goods would be given preference. Domestic production would be encouraged.

Tracy remembered how the paper had provided massive support to her election campaign. But she was also aware how rocky the subsequent road had been. In public, she presented a self-confident image, following a resolutely proactive policy. She believed implicitly in the destiny of her country. After all, many nations were economically successful without being part of an economic bloc. And few of them possessed Britain's advantages, with her industrial history, well known service industries, a language spoken throughout the world and her unparalleled global historical ties.

But privately Tracy experienced moments of hesitation, known only to herself, and even terrors which woke her in the night. Walks calmed her down.

She passed the Savoy. The superb hotel, opened in 1889, at the height of the British Empire, was her favourite place for meetings over tea. The building, crowned with a Union Jack atop a tall flagpole, was lavishly illuminated, brightly visible through the trees from the Embankment in this winter season. She amused herself trying to pick out, amongst all the glittering windows, the small dining room where she was often seated, but without success.

London's beauty still amazed her even after all these years. This city has stood firm through so many trials, she thought, revolutions, the Great Fire of 1666, the Blitz, and today it is truly majestic. Her optimism returned. Just like its capital, the country would find a solution to its problems, as always.

Following the planned route, she crossed Waterloo Bridge and went back along the Thames on the other bank. She watched the boats coming and going, and heard the seagull cries again. She slipped through the throngs of pedestrians. She listened to the living, breathing sound of London. She returned peacefully to Downing Street, with a lighter heart.

Monsieur Marquet has a problem

On the other side of the Channel, in the Elysée Palace, President Edouard Marquet, his back turned to his desk, looked out of the window at an empty garden, the trees covered with a light dusting of frost, under a grey and sullen winter sky. Mulling over the last five years, he was anxiously aware of the impending deadline of the presidential elections of May 2022 and the subsequent parliamentary elections. Despite his efforts, France's economic situation had not fundamentally improved over the course of his presidency. First of all, contrary to his expectations, the country had not benefited from Britain's hard Brexit. While some financial institutions had chosen to relocate to Paris after leaving London, the majority had chosen Frankfurt, Dublin, Luxembourg or other cities. French industry had not been able to take advantage of the withdrawal of its English competitors; the situation had benefited either Germany, whose industry was better prepared to take on additional production, or countries such as Spain or Eastern Europe, which were less expensive than France. Moreover, the sharp decline in European exports to the United Kingdom after Brexit had crippled French businesses, while the Germans had been able to absorb the shock thanks to their greater exposure to world markets. The tourism sector had seen a notable decline in British visitors, farming subsidies had dropped because of the reduction in the European budget, and pharmaceutical laboratories had suffered from increased British competition. In short, there were few sectors that had benefited from the situation. The truth was that Brexit had had a lasting negative impact on the French economy.

Moreover, the economic, social and institutional reforms that the French President had courageously brought in, sometimes with difficulty, had had only limited effect in the context of very strong international competition: the country remained too expensive compared to the Asian giants. Efforts to reduce labour costs had led to less job security for workers without creating new jobs at the rate predicted. The digital revolution, which had been generating large scale transformation over the last few years, created new opportunities, which the President had strongly encouraged and where France performed to advantage, but at the cost of a merciless annihilation of many types of job, widening the social divide. The government remained in chronic deficit, the national debt, dangerously high, was expensive because of the rise in interest rates. And finally, the security situation remained very tense because of Islamist terrorism.

The electoral campaign was anticipated to be very difficult. In 2017, Marquet had won by selling the voters on a new method of politics, promising to govern with a pragmatic approach beyond the usual party political divides. His approach had succeeded beyond all expectations. He had not only been elected, but the party he had created in a few months had won a very large majority in Parliament, shattering all the alliances opposed to him. In 2022, he would have to compete in a very different context. It would no longer be possible for him to present himself as a new man, and he and his party would have to defend their track record against attacks from all sides.

The French political landscape was dangerously fragmented. On the ruins of the parties which had collapsed in 2017, five significant movements had sprung up, three to the right of the president's party, two to his left, six parties in total, not to mention many small groups spread across the electoral spectrum. Votes would therefore be divided across a very wide offering, making any forecasts highly uncertain.

The European issue was one of the main areas of political debate albeit in a new light compared to previous elections, because of the positions taken by several of the parties. In fact, at both extremes of the political spectrum, there were movements which, for opposite reasons, wanted France to free itself from the constraints of the European Union: the right wing wanted to adopt a policy focusing on intense protectionism and security, with border controls incompatible with the rules of the single market; the left wing wanted to embark on a policy of high expenditure and reform of the social model, on a basis that would exceed the prudent management rules of public finances laid out in the treaties on the single currency. These two parties were both critical of the "unbridled capitalism" which according to them had been cultivated by European rules on open competition. Their arguments resonated to a certain extent with voters. Their manifestos therefore provided for a negotiation phase with the country's European partners followed by referendums on an exit from the European Union in the event of failure. Loath to be left behind, the right-wing Republicans had also put a referendum on a new European treaty in their manifesto, claiming the need to restore sovereignty to the nations of Europe.

European issues had been unexpectedly absent from the President's policy during his tenure, apart from his tough opposition to the United Kingdom in the Brexit negotiations. His European colleagues had not been much more active. Of course, following the outcome of the British referendum, the political world of mainland Europe had been shaken, and had talked about what reforms were necessary to revive the European project and to counteract its democratic deficit. A great many impressive speeches had been made, including those of the French president. He had set out ambitious proposals. But five years on, nothing had changed. Germany, paralysed by internal policy conflicts, remained unconvinced by the French proposals, but had not come up with an alternative vision. Across other countries, frankly divergent positions had been taken. President Marquet, soon absorbed in his own domestic difficulties, had had to give up on the leadership role he had initially been ambitious for. The Brussels bureaucracies, on the other hand, in an attempt to reduce the impression, even if unwarranted, of governing Europe, had scaled back their initiatives. The British vote had smoothly been passed off as the eccentric decision of an insular people who had foolishly been granted a risky referendum. It had also been supposed that the obvious difficulties of Brexit would serve as a deterrent to the populations of other countries. The debate had petered out, and in the absence of a strong political will, Europe had not moved forward.

Marquet was belatedly beginning to understand the fundamental problem that this posed in the current political situation. If the French electorate was seduced by the proposals from some parties for leaving Europe, Europe would not survive: a "Frexit", added to Brexit, would sound the death knell of any kind of European project. This scenario could not be ruled out, given the electoral situation and the uncertainty of any referendum.

Even worse, France's situation was not unique: political fragmentation had continued in many countries, fuelled by popular discontent. Support for parties hostile to the development of Europe was growing steadily. Several governments had now been subjected to disciplinary proceedings by the European institutions for breaches of the Treaties. The general situation was becoming tense. The European Union was on the verge of exploding.

Marquet wanted to win the next election, for his country, for himself and for the image that he wanted to leave for posterity. He refused to give way to parties that he believed would drag France and Europe into the abyss. He vowed to find a solution, but he only had a few months left to do it.

Sovereignty

At the beginning of January, John Klin, a Professor at the London School of Economics, had an article published in a weekend newspaper.

"Europe's great mistake has been to believe that a nation can give up sovereignty. That is not possible. If a nation exists, it is because the individuals who comprise it recognise it as the relevant frame of reference for their collective representation.

"The citizen's requirement is that his situation be better with the nation than without it. If that contract does not exist, if doubt creeps in, the nation falls apart. Where, in particular, a segment of the population identifies first and foremost with a new frame of reference – their area or region, for example – the nation runs the risk of schism. That is why a nation must be strong to ensure its cohesion. In this balancing act, surrender of sovereignty to a supranational entity can never be a winning bet. If the supranational entity is not credible, citizens will not accept it being given powers. And if on the contrary it is more credible than the nation, it means that the nation cannot remain the frame of reference for its citizens. This is an existential question for nations. Governments that negotiate treaties containing delegation of decision-making run the almost certain risk of not being followed by the people they represent.

"If nations are not prepared to abandon their sovereignty, that is not to say that they cannot make compromises. They can accept limits on their freedom, in the context of negotiations with their partners, if these limits are contractual, justified and reversible. Europe, to be successful, must be based on these foundations. A technocratic delegation of power is possible, on the dual condition of remaining under the political control of the delegating nations and demonstrating its benefits.

"The United States of Europe cannot exist until citizens recognise Europe as their relevant frame of reference. As this recognition clearly does not exist today, it is not possible to create institutions on this model, not even forerunners of institutions on this model. The European Parliament consequently lacks the necessary legitimacy to carry out its functions: it cannot legislate in the name of the nations, because it does not represent them (national parliaments do), nor can it be under the control of the governments, which would be incompatible with its Parliamentary function. Consequently it can neither be the legislator nor the instrument of the European project. Therefore, it can be, at best, a floor for discussion and exchange. The European Commission, on the other hand, as a technocratic structure, can function without contradiction, provided that it is under the political control of the nations.

"If Europe is based on the above model, it can function effectively and be recognised as legitimate by its citizens.

"This reasoning is obviously open to criticism from supporters of a proactive European project. "What powers would a European framework constantly subject to the nations have?" they may object. "How could we impose decisions beneficial to the common good? How could we build Europe without relinquishing sovereignty?"

"The starting point of this argument is the analysis that if each European decision is to be subject to validation at a national level, nothing will progress, or at any rate, nothing will progress uniformly. But this argument can immediately be countered: what is the point of progress if it is against the will of the citizens involved? Europe was built for the benefit of its citizens. If they do not recognize the value of a given decision, what is the legitimacy of these decisions? And if they do recognize them, what is the problem with letting nations approve these decisions? Furthermore, for more effective decision-making, it is not necessarily a question of having each new rule approved, but of allowing the ruling nations to veto it within a given time. A multi-speed Europe could emerge in this model, because some nations will not adopt all the rules; however, this is a strength rather than a weakness: the flexibility thus gained allows nations so wishing to move forward quickly on specific topics.

"The other objection that can be made is: "It is wrong to restrict the citizen's adherence to a single frame of reference. A citizen can identify with his local council for local matters, his region for regional topics, his country for national issues, and to the European Union for supranational problems. A concept of European citizenship has been created, which is widely appreciated by Europeans". In fact this is not even an objection. The model proposed in this article does not contradict the existence of several levels of governance. A citizen can recognise multiple levels of administrative bodies, complying with the principles of subsidiarity. What a citizen will not accept, and this goes to the heart of our discussion, is the fact that a supranational body can take decisions that affect the daily lives of citizens, without the supervision of local decision-making bodies. The citizen rightly sees this as a deviation from the role of the supranational body, whose exclusive mandate, according to the citizen, is to resolve matters of general interest where it is better placed to do so than the local authorities, but within the framework of a controlled delegation of powers.

"A European Union model which respects the nations is much more robust than a centralising model. Human nature abhors a void, or an imbalance. If we try to centralise the decision-making process, some citizens will immediately start applying centrifugal force. The more we try to centralise, the stronger the centrifugal force. If, conversely, there is no, or minimal centralisation, inverse forces are generated. So there is a pragmatic interest in implementing a model for building Europe which is more flexible and more respectful of national authorities.

"What citizens reject is not the European project. Most people understand the value of close cooperation between countries, harmonisation and simplification of trade procedures, and a collective defence of certain fundamental interests against a world that is increasingly dominated by giant economies. Europeans also accept the construction of a cultural space bringing together broadly similar countries who respect common values – and thus a form of European citizenship. What the majority of citizens reject, and what has led to Brexit, is the perceived deviation of European institutions from the mandate for which they, or so we believe, were created, when decisions contrary to the interests of their nation can be taken by a majority decision without national supervision.

"If Europe is able to restructure how it functions, it would not be impossible for British citizens to reconsider their vote. A political party proposing this new European contract could, in due course, form a government. The United Kingdom could extricate itself from its current dead-end position."

"John Klin, January 8th, 2022, London."

It was above all the last sentence of John Klin's article which led to much debate. The Labour leader questioned the Prime Minister in Parliament the following week: "If Europe changes its model, will the Prime Minister propose the United Kingdom's re-entry into the European Union on a sovereign nation basis?"

In asking the question, Jones knew perfectly well the answer he would get. His intention was to clearly delineate his political difference.

Tracy Meller, as expected, replied in the negative: "Firstly, this is not the current position, so the question is rhetorical. The European Union has not reformed its institutions. Secondly, even if it did, forty years of experience have clearly shown us its political and technocratic procedures. We know that other key nations do not have the same vision as Britain of the Union's final objective. Even with more protective institutional changes, we would be caught up again in the onerous decision-making processes of an organization composed of 28 members. Our citizens have understandably chosen freedom. This freedom will lead to the success of our country."

Jones took careful note of the answer. He knew that the Prime Minister was not able to reply any differently, without reneging on her own policies of the last five years, and without risking a break-up of her party. But he also knew that her answer had demonstrated how she was increasingly out of step with public opinion, which, slowly but surely, was starting to widely believe that the current situation was not tenable, and that sooner or later, the whole country would have to draw that conclusion.

A Serious Alert

Public opinion had it that Philip Denniel, Governor of the Bank of England for the last two years, was being paid to do nothing. It was true that he had not changed the interest rate, which was at zero when he took office. The public did not see his technical work, which took place behind the scenes, trying to save the banking system, secure liquidity in the economy, and support the faltering markets. As the interest rate did not change, inflation continued to grow and the pound continued to depreciate, people concluded that the Bank of England was useless and that Denniel was at least in part responsible for the current economic woes. The Christmas pudding he had received in the face was certainly down to this reputation.

But Philip Denniel was a seasoned economist. A former corporate banker, he had amassed a substantial fortune that he had had the foresight to convert to dollars just before the Brexit vote, the outcome of which he had predicted exactly despite widespread belief in the opposite result coming to pass. He lived in pricey Chelsea, where he had bought a house, with his wife and two daughters. He was a bearded, physically imposing man of fifty-five, with a tranquil nature, liking nothing better than ruminating as he smoked his pipe or walked his Labrador.

His abilities were acknowledged in the financial world. He had been appointed urgently to the helm of the Bank when his predecessor, exasperated by government policy, stormed out at the end of 2019, declaring that he was no longer prepared to stand surety for a suicidal policy.

Denniel liked discretion. He had discussed the situation at length during hushed meetings with the main economic players and then had begun to act, working on a cautious technical basis. Experts recognized that up till now he had saved the country's economy from a major crisis. But they also declared, and this statement was what the public remembered, that the macroeconomic situation was not improving, and that the financial situation could collapse at any time.

On Tuesday, January 11th, 2022, Denniel received alarming warnings. Three major banks had applied for emergency assistance in the face of a run of withdrawals. The Governor was also informed of massive positioning on the financial markets hedging on a new currency devaluation. Speculators were at work.

As if by chance, articles had appeared in the newspapers before and after the last weekend of the year, calling on people to look to their savings in view of a forthcoming severe crisis. Around noon, panic seized the markets and the stock market index dropped by six percent. Denniel conferred with the Chancellor of the Exchequer and the Prime Minister. Statements were made; the Bank of England pledged to put up unlimited funds to prevent a financial crisis.

This announcement, which normally produced the desired result, had only a partial effect. When the markets closed, the situation remained extremely tense.

The following day, January 12th, the Bank of England carried out a significant intervention. This was one of the most difficult days of the past two years for the Governor. Apart from another appearance on television to reassure investors, he remained closeted all day with his advisory team, having a sandwich lunch, taking decisions after rapid deliberations over the latest developments. It proved necessary to support a number of financial institutions, to undertake massive purchases and to use the currency reserves to shore up the pound. The Prime Minister made a statement to confirm that the Government was taking all appropriate measures. By that evening the situation began to ease. Savers had been somewhat reassured and the speculators had relaxed their grip on the markets.

On 13th January, Denniel saw financial activity returning to normal, and a moderate recovery of stock exchange prices. By the end of the week, the crisis was over. The shock had been severe and had consumed a significant portion of the bank's resources. The markets had taken a serious hit. The governor knew that if another crisis occurred in the near future, he would have limited room for manoeuvre and the consequences could be much more dramatic.

The BBC Interviews

During the third week of January 2022, the BBC broadcast a series of interviews with members of the British public, explaining how Brexit had affected them.

The first person interviewed was the owner of a tea room, Elisabeth, an unmarried woman aged about forty. Elisabeth had voted without hesitation for Brexit. The BBC asked her if she regretted her vote now.

"Not in the slightest," she replied. "Before the vote, there were two competing cafes in my street, one Polish and one Spanish. Both have closed down. People have gone back to their old ways. What could be more British than a tea room? I was having trouble getting enough customers in. Now customers are meeting here happily."

The reporter questioned her further: "Isn't that reducing customer choice? Before they could choose from three places and now there's only one?"

"Maybe," replied Elisabeth. "But what did that choice cost us? British unemployment. If things had gone on as they were, I would have had to close down and lay off my staff because I wasn't getting anywhere. I would have had to put more people on the dole, while my competitors sent money back to their countries."

"Why were they doing better than you?"

"They attracted all the immigrants from their own community, and Brits who went there to try something exotic. But mostly it was because they paid their staff less and fiddled their National Insurance."

"Did their cafes compete with you on quality?"

"They weren't as good as my tea room. They had a much simpler niche."

"Why did they shut down?"

"They were afraid of the consequences of the Brexit vote. They thought they would be thrown out. They preferred to pre-empt that and invest in their own country."

"There are Indian restaurants in your town. Don't you mind that competition?"

"It's not the same thing. They aren't cafes. And anyway we're used to them, they've been here longer. And they speak English."

"Didn't the other cafe owners speak English?"

"Oh no, hardly at all!" (Elisabeth bursts out laughing.) "You couldn't understand a word they said. There should be language tests before you're allowed to settle in a country."

"If the government decided to rejoin the European Economic Area or the European Union, how would you react?"

"I'd go to Westminster, and I'd camp there, millions of us English would, until they gave up on it."

"But what if this decision was the result of a vote of the majority of the population?"

"That won't happen," Elisabeth finished firmly.

The second interview was with a mechanic, John Treble. A forty-five-year-old father of two children, he had also voted for Brexit. But he regretted his choice.

"I voted leave, because of the foreigners, and the constantly increasing regulation. All that was driving me crazy, and I put it down to Brussels. But at the end of the day nothing has changed, there's no less red tape, and even if there are fewer Europeans coming here, the number of immigrants from other countries has increased just as much, no matter what the government says. The politicians lied to us. My costs have risen enormously because I import a lot of parts, and people just haven't got the cash for it any more. My takings have really dropped since Brexit. That lot in Westminster, who told us how to vote, they still get paid whatever."

"But now that people are buying more vehicles manufactured in Britain, isn't that good for your business? You can buy locally made parts."

"Even British made parts are more expensive than before. We haven't gained anything."

"How old are your children?"

"Seventeen and fourteen, both boys."

"What do they think about how you voted?"

"They blame me for it. They both want to study abroad, at least for a few years. It's a lot harder since Brexit, and too expensive for me. My boys say that when they are old enough to vote, their generation will demand a new referendum."

"If the government decided to return to the European Economic Area or the European Union, how would you react?"

"Big round of applause from me. I'd vote for the party that proposes that, whoever they are."

The third interviewee, Mark Steward, was a professor at Oxford University. Aged thirty-five, he had voted Remain. But now he was seeing some positive results of Brexit in his field.

"I didn't vote to leave the European Union. The European ideal is a beautiful concept, and I am in favour of it. But with the pound's drop in value, we've had an influx of foreign students. The English educational system is a gold standard worldwide. As a result of our increased revenue, the university now has much more money than it did five years ago, especially as the government has increased grants for scientific research. A lot of researchers come to see us from other countries and are amazed by our facilities. Even though there are still gaps to be filled, this is something that five years ago would have been unthinkable. However, to be clear: this new prosperity is a result of the value of the pound, not the fact that we are outside the European Union. We should have found our way to a different agreement, and negotiated more regulatory and economic freedom, without leaving Europe. University exchanges between countries have been made more difficult since Brexit. Foreigners are coming here, but our students can't go abroad because of the cost. In the long run, we are going to suffer."

"What do you think is the priority: to continue to strengthen our education system or enable our young people to go abroad to study?"

"They are not mutually exclusive; we should not have to choose. Welcoming foreign students to our universities allows us to access funds that will help make our education system more efficient. But we should also work to renew our international partnerships and create scholarships to send students from the young generation to other countries. That cross fertilisation is necessary."

"I'll ask you the question that we are putting to all our interviewees: if the government decided to rejoin the European Economic Area or the European Union, how would you react?"

"I would be very much in favour, provided that it is accompanied by reasonable conditions for our country."

Mrs Laura Caleigh, sixty years old, a former bank manager, was the fourth person interviewed. Mrs Caleigh had been forced into early retirement by her bank a year after Brexit, as part of a move to relocate activities abroad. In her interview with the BBC, she immediately indicated her anti-Brexit opinions.

"I always thought that this vote was a massive mistake. Our financial sector was the best in Europe. You only had to look at the City and Canary Wharf at rush hour: a real hive of industry, with employees from all over the world. Walk round Canary Wharf today: it's half empty. Some buildings are no longer even maintained. The employees have been let go. The banks have moved their operations abroad; they took the opportunity to save money because London's wages, which were justified in the boom time, had become unaffordable after the financial crisis. It's also not economically feasible to carry out Euro operations from London – there are too many barriers and complications. Our industry has taken a terrible hit from devaluation, low rates, and an increase in bankruptcy amongst borrowers. Many of our major banks are now in a difficult financial situation, and it wouldn't take much for them to go under. And all for what? What have we actually gained out of this? A bit more competitiveness and freedom for our country? What does that amount to, up against the Asian giants?"

"Do you think this was all predictable?"

"Most of the economic analyses done before the referendum gave warnings about the consequences. People didn't want to believe them."

"Isn't Brexit an opportunity to refocus the British economy on real industrial bases, on a firm foundation of reinvigorated competitiveness? In other words, to create an economy for the benefit of the whole country, rather than a small elite in London?"

"We have been predominantly a nation of traders and financiers for generations. The primary requirement for these two activities is access to the surrounding markets. If it ain't broke, don't fix it! As for the new basis of the economy you mentioned, it hasn't succeeded, with a few rare exceptions."

"If the government decided to rejoin the European Economic Area or the European Union, how would you react?"

"I'd be really relieved. It's too late for me. I won't find another job at my age. But for the younger generation, it would mean new opportunities. Our young people are well educated and enterprising; they have nothing to fear from exposure to the European market, quite the opposite. They will reap enormous benefits."

The fifth interview was with Mr James, a barrister, at his Chambers. Six years ago, then thirty years old, he had been an active Leave campaigner, handing out leaflets in the streets, approaching passers-by, convincing them one by one. Today he has not gone back on any of his beliefs.

"2016 was a historic year. Of course it was, and is still, difficult. Birth never happens without pain. But our nation has regained its identity. Our government can legislate without interference. European law no longer applies here. We use English common law, so well adapted to the circumstances of our country. Immigration has also significantly dropped, and our once-threatened traditions have been strengthened."

"Do you think these changes justify the economic price being paid by the country at the moment?"

"There were crises before Brexit and there will be again. This is nothing new. Remember the crisis of 2008, which was more serious than the one we have been going through for the last few years. The difference is that now we have our own decision-making capacity to address our problems. The debate has been simplified: no one has to wonder if Brussels is responsible for the difficult situation. These days, if there is a problem, it is up to the government to solve it; it can't abdicate its responsibilities anymore."

"What would you say to the Scots who, according to the opinion polls, want independence in order to rejoin Europe?"

"I'd tell them to think carefully. Why choose union with distant and technocratic governance, when the majority of Scotland's economic trade is with England?"

"Our usual question: if the government decided to rejoin the European Economic Area or the European Union, how would you react?"

"I'd go back onto the streets, with my old leaflets!"

Meeting between Tracy Meller and Philip Denniel

Since becoming Prime Minister, Tracy Meller had always ensured that she had regular meetings with the Governor of the Bank of England. It was true that the Bank had to maintain an obligatory independence from the government, but this did not prevent them from having a close relationship. Government departments had frequent meetings with the Bank. Tracy also wanted to keep ongoing direct contact at the highest level.

These meetings were often held over tea in a private dining room at the Savoy Hotel, which provided the Prime Minister with a beautiful and discreet setting.

Today's topic was an important one. Shaken by the financial crisis in early January, Tracy was convinced that a new assault on the market was brewing and was anxious to prepare an adequate response. She had briefed the Chancellor of the Exchequer, but also wanted to discuss it personally with the Governor.

His words did not reassure her: 2022 was looking difficult for many reasons. First of all the economic upturn, so frequently promised and awaited by the government, was still not in sight.

In addition, this year would see the end of some of the provisional measures negotiated for four years with the European Union in 2018. Because of the legal vacuum created by the lack of agreement between Britain and Europe, London and Brussels had at the time agreed on some practical provisions to reduce the complications of exit, and to mitigate the mutual impact. Among these provisions was an agreement guaranteeing the continuity of residence status for European workers in Great Britain and those of the British in the European Union. Without calling the legal basis into question, and in particular without authorising new settlements, this agreement had the merit of avoiding an overly abrupt relocation of the citizens concerned. Many other technical provisions were in a similar situation, for example mutual acceptance of medical products on the basis of national tests, which had been essential for the British pharmaceutical industry. The renegotiation of these transitional provisions before they expired this year would generate political and economic uncertainties.

On the other hand, the Governor pointed out, 2022 was an election year in several countries and especially in France, where the rise of extreme parties was perceived very negatively by economists and bankers. If one of these parties were to be elected, its policy would be quite likely to result in France's exit from the Eurozone and the European Union, with violently negative effects on the international situation. In Germany, something of a slowdown in the industrial model had been observed, intensified by the country's structural problems such as its demographic decline, and immigration-related tensions. More generally, the Governor pointed to ongoing weak areas within the Eurozone that had still not been resolved. Growth had resumed in Asia and America, raising fears of capital investment being diverted to these regions rather than Europe or Britain. Finally, the threat of another Scottish independence referendum added to the uncertainty. Taken together, these factors could lead to a very tense few months for the markets in early 2022, as had been demonstrated by the mini-crisis in January.

Now the ability of the Government and the Bank of England to respond had been greatly diminished. Foreign exchange reserves had declined over the last five years. With interest rates already at zero, there was no possibility of lowering them to revive the economy and this was driving a price rise. The Bank of England's balance sheet, inflated by a heavy buying policy over several years, would not permit any more large-scale measures and needed to be reduced as soon as possible. The country's debt had grown significantly. And with inflation and economic hardship, the country's credit had dwindled and its borrowing capacity could be affected. The bond markets were beginning to express doubts about the UK's ability to meet its obligations without restructuring. Instead of being able to maintain interest rates at their current level, the Bank of England would soon be under pressure to increase them, which would penalise the economy. In concluding his summing up of the situation, the Governor reminded the Prime Minister that the measures taken during the crisis on January 11th had used up some of the last available room for manoeuvre.

Tracy felt very tense listening to the Governor. She was not unaware of these problems. But the Governor's concise summary had something particularly terrifying about it. All the ingredients for a financial powder keg were assembled and the authorities had no means to deal with it. But she would not allow herself to be beaten down. She steered the conversation towards the best technical decisions to take, given the constraints, in the event that a major crisis hit the markets. When she left the Governor, she would have liked nothing better than to walk back to Downing Street. But it was raining hard and she had to give up on the idea. That night, she slept badly. She could not know, however, that the major crisis she feared, the crisis that would change the very future of the country – and her own – was only a few days away.

The HGB Bank

Laura Soriens had been Chief Executive of the HGB Bank (Holtmington, Gratestley & Brothers) for three years. This position, at the helm of one of the oldest English financial institutions, was the culmination of a brilliant career. An Oxford graduate, Laura had begun her professional career at the Treasury, where she had stayed for ten years. She had then worked at the International Monetary Fund in the United States for five years. After a brief stint at an investment bank in New York, she decided to return to England after the 2008 crisis, when she was forty years old, to raise her two children in their home country. Hired as HGB's Investment Director, she worked her way up and was appointed to the position of Chief Executive in 2019, at fifty-one.

Laura Soriens had a strong personality. Outgoing and approachable, she was a great conversationalist, spending hours chatting with myriad contacts. That was her strength, which enabled her to keep abreast of everything. As comfortable with a Board of Directors as with the bank's most junior staff, she knew how to charm those around her, while being very demanding of her colleagues. Her knowledge of the trade and her experience were acknowledged.

However, the role of Chief Executive had disconcerted her. Having previously undertaken predominantly technical positions, she discovered that her new role was responsible for a host of duties which had little to do with the core banking business. Issues of compliance with the endless rules, meetings with regulatory authorities, HR matters, or discussions with trades unions, took a considerable amount of time, not to mention Audit Committees, Boards, presentations to investors, and hordes of other inescapable meetings. She was also regularly invited to the Treasury for them to hear her opinion and that of her peers on "the best steps to take to strengthen the country's economy". She ended up wondering what role she played in managing the bank, given how little time she had to do it. She was glad she could rely on competent colleagues who took the necessary day-to-day decisions. She knew, however, that the day there was a serious problem, she would be on the front line.

That day had come.

The bank had experienced difficult times in recent years. Brexit had obliged it to restructure. Whole departments linked to European markets had been relocated to the Eurozone. The bank was then faced with bankrupt borrowers and its margins were severely squeezed by the economic situation. Redundancies had to be made. All this had been started under Soriens's predecessor and she continued the policy. The bank had been doing better over the last two years, even though it had never recovered its pre-Brexit health. However, the brief crisis in January had shaken it.

On Friday 28th January 2022, Mr Hector, the CFO, came to see the Chief Executive. With his nose in his files, he told her that he had just received the provisional accounts of the Construct company for 2021. Its financial statements showed a colossal loss, greater than the company's own funds.

"Construct is going to be declared bankrupt," said Mr Hector. "The shareholders can't afford to recapitalise."

Laura Soriens closed her eyes for a moment. Construct going bankrupt meant a loss of one and a half billion pounds for HGB.

"Our auditors are insisting that we provision our risk at 100%," continued Mr Hector. "We provisioned five hundred million last June, so we have to make up the difference in our end-of-year accounts."

The Construct company had been a long-time customer of HGB. Founded in 1980 as a construction company, it had diversified into property after 2000. It had been a big player in the development of London and other English cities, building skyscrapers, blocks of flats, offices and infrastructure. Caught up in over-expansion, Construct had bought its main competitor in 2014, borrowing several billion pounds. Brexit was a rude shock. A number of major developments, which it had financed by borrowing, no longer found buyers despite declining prices. The company, which was then risking considerable losses, had the idea of using the pound's weakness to attract a foreign clientele, especially Asians and Americans, who would be able to take advantage of the exchange rate to invest at a good price, while relying on a medium-term market recovery after the initial shock of Brexit. For the first two years, the idea worked, thanks to the commercial dynamism of the sales teams. Construct succeeded in selling some of its developments, and, boosted by a new optimism and the rescheduling of its debt with the banks, even embarked on new ones. From 2020, however, the enthusiasm of foreign investors dried up, when the British economic difficulties showed no signs of coming to an end. Hopes for a market recovery were fading, and the progressive depreciation of the pound led to losses for the buyers. Construct's problems took a dramatic turn at the end of the year when the American Treasury accused the company of money laundering and illicit trade in dollars. Because of its aggressive marketing strategy, Construct had not been strict enough on the origins of its buyers' money. The investigation revealed that the source of some investors' funds was linked to drug trafficking or illegal arms sales. After a thorough investigation, the US authorities imposed a huge fine on Construct in September 2021. The company was also the subject of numerous lawsuits by investors whose developments were not delivered on time due to financial difficulties. Still theoretically solvent at the end of 2020, the company was at bay by the end of 2021. Sales had entirely ground to a halt and liabilities clearly exceeded the assets. Over the years, Construct's shareholders had restructured the shareholdings, and it turned out some of these funds were domiciled in tax havens. Hidden behind these shell funds, the original owners of the group had become untouchable. As the company could not count on an injection of capital to pay off its debts, bankruptcy was inevitable.

HGB had lent a great deal of money to Construct since the year 2000, certainly more than was prudent, and, going from restructure to restructure, had never succeeded in significantly reducing its exposure despite its growing worries. The bank found itself risking considerable losses, much higher than the acceptable maximum under its official policy of exposure management. Although of course it could seize part of Construct's property holdings, it knew that under current market conditions it would be very difficult to get much money for it. On the other hand, winding up Construct would take a long time and the distribution of assets between creditors would be the subject of lengthy legal proceedings. So HGB's auditors had good reason to advise provisioning the maximum amount of losses.

The Construct issue had obviously been highly publicised over the last few months, especially after the American fine. The company's bankruptcy would have a political impact, in addition to its financial consequences. The government would be accused of failures in supervision. As for HGB, the loss, coupled with the bank's existing difficulties, would hit the accounts heavily, and they would veer well into the red. However, Laura Soriens was more concerned about the reaction of minor savers and shareholders, who would accuse HGB of reckless risk-taking. A crisis of confidence was to be expected. The bank's stock market price would collapse and the customers, in a moment of panic made worse by the general economic climate, would rush to withdraw their deposits in their droves. The Director discussed the situation with Mr Hector, who confirmed that he had already given instructions for liquidity funds to be obtained urgently from the central Bank and other financial institutions. However, they both knew that it would be difficult because several other banks on the market had significant exposure to Construct. When their meeting ended, the CFO picked up his bundles of files and left the office, and Laura Soriens convened her executive committee for an extraordinary meeting within the next hour.

In the meantime, she telephoned the Chairman of the bank to inform him of the situation and the arrangements to be made. The subject of Construct was not a new topic of conversation for either of these two executives. But there is a big difference between forecasting bad news and getting full confirmation of it and all its consequences, when there are already a hundred other difficult issues to deal with. The Chief Executive and the Chairman tried to find an appropriate response to a problem that they knew would poison the bank for months. They were expecting a media feeding frenzy, questions from everywhere – employees, the Audit Committee, the Board, the regulatory authorities, the press... Plenty of people would be keen to tell them what they ought to have done, implying that if they had been in charge, the problem would never have occurred.

Soriens thought about David Cameron, who had received a different type of catastrophic news – the Brexit referendum result – for which he had had to assume full responsibility. She offered the Chairman her resignation; he refused, saying that she was not responsible for the Construct file, which she had inherited on her appointment (the more cynical truth was that the Chairman wished to keep the Director on the front line and keep his powder dry for her resignation at a later stage). Soriens proposed that as the best line of defence is attack, they would have to publicly blame the government for its lack of oversight of Construct. The Chairman dissuaded her from that line of strategy, firstly because he was close to the Prime Minister, and secondly because accusing the government would not exonerate the bank from its responsibilities as they had willingly loaned considerable sums of money to Construct. The two executives agreed to stick to a technical and reassuring line: the losses had been provisioned as a precaution but were not yet proven, the bank could stand them, there would be funds from the seized property assets, the liquidity ratios would remain well over the regulatory minimum.

It was agreed that Laura Soriens would ring the Governor of the Bank of England to inform him of the latest developments, while the Chairman contacted the Prime Minister.

After this discussion, the Chief Executive convened her Executive Committee. The Chairman phoned Tracy Meller, then, deciding that the circumstances did not warrant him living like a pauper, went to lunch at his favourite luxurious riverside restaurant.

As soon as he had sat down in the sitting room which was kept reserved for him, he dialled a number on his secure line:

"Luke," he said quietly.

"Yes, boss?"

"Construct is going under. Our master plan starts next week. Prepare our friends for a massive sell off on the markets. But be careful, wait for me to give the word. We'll need to see how the government reacts at the beginning of the week."

"Got it, boss."

The Chairman rang off just as the waiter came in with his exquisite lobster salad, a speciality of the establishment.

Tracy Meller discovers the collapse of Construct

If there was an event which Tracy Meller could have well done without, it was the bankruptcy of Construct. After the phone call from the Chairman of HGB, around 11:30 on the morning of Friday 28th January, she found herself envisaging Jeremy Jones at the next sitting of Parliament, accusing the Government of rank incompetence. He would hold her directly responsible for the losses incurred by the investors who had put their trust in Construct, by the small shareholders of the banks whose shares would fall, and by the employees who would lose their jobs. In particular, he would draw the obvious conclusion – the failure of "Brexit XXL", under which historic flagships of the British economy like Construct and HGB were doomed to go down.

Tracy was not too worried about the debate in Parliament. The often rowdy discussions that took place there were unpleasant, but generally had few political consequences, were ignored or quickly forgotten by the public. What troubled her was that there would be a good bit of truth in Jones' arguments. The failure of Construct was first and foremost the result of a very aggressive strategy. But it was undeniable that Brexit XXL had hit the company hard. If the UK had at least remained in the EEA, the property market would not have been in such severe crisis, and the pound would not have dropped so much in value. The British banks, and HGB in particular, would not have gone through the considerable difficulties they had been experiencing for five years. All of these companies had been flourishing in 2016. The banks had strengthened their equity funds after the financial crisis of 2008 and even if the economic situation at the time had caused some problems, they were much better positioned than their competitors in Europe. London's financial centre was the best in Europe. Construct's aggressive strategy was understandable, in the context of the growth of the British, and in particular, the London, economy at the time. The rates were low so it was not unreasonable to borrow. If it had not been for Brexit, these companies would probably now be the pride of Britain.

Tracy also thought about the employees who would lose their jobs: Construct employed thousands who would soon be unemployed without hope of finding another job in the near future. She spent a good part of the day discussing the consequences of the bankruptcy with the Chancellor of the Exchequer. She also had a conference call with the Governor of the Bank of England. They both shared their fears of disastrous consequences during the week to come, when the news was made public. Tracy decided to have a long discussion on the subject at an emergency Cabinet meeting on Monday and sent instructions to that end. She made it known that she would make a public announcement on Tuesday morning.

★ ★ ★

At about five o'clock, she went out for a walk in St James's Park. It was raining slightly, a fine cold drizzle, but she was well covered. The freshness did her good. With her headscarf on, she was hardly recognisable by passers-by, especially in the dim light of this time of day. She was followed as usual by two bodyguards in plain clothes. She had chosen to walk along the little lake. The park's elegance, its greenery, its squirrels and ducks, always made it a lovely place for a walk. She spotted two tramps lying on a bench, protected from the rain by a plastic sheet. The two bodyguards closed the gap with her immediately, but the men were sleeping deeply. Tracy continued on. Had she become involved in politics and taken on the position of Prime Minister, only for this to happen? She had campaigned about improving the lot of ordinary people. She had promised to make Brexit a success for Great Britain. Now, it was the ordinary people who were suffering, the employees who had lost their jobs, small scale investors who were seeing their savings evaporate. How many would end up on the streets, like those poor homeless men?

Tracy was a fighter. She rarely let events get the better of her. But today she was painfully aware of her powerlessness. For the first time, she wondered seriously if she might have taken a wrong turn.

Leaving the lake, she went back up the slope that leads to the Mall. From there she had a view of Buckingham Palace, majestic and imperturbable in the drizzle. The Foot Guards stood still. A few tourists with umbrellas were taking pictures. The Royal Standard was flying, showing the Queen was at home. What did the Queen really think? Tracy saw her every week, in private, in spite of the sovereign's declining health, to keep her informed of political developments. In public, the Queen had never spoken in favour of Brexit, or against it, for that matter. The Queen could not interfere in politics and uttering an opinion on a topic that was so divisive for her subjects would have fanned the flames of dissent dangerously. But even in the entirely confidential setting of their meetings, she had never confided to her Prime Minister on this issue. Tracy, however, had an inkling of what she thought. Despite the sovereign's formidable ability to remain impassive and control her emotions, she let slip certain clues. What the Prime Minister guessed at was this: the Queen did not necessarily have a very favourable opinion of Brussels and its technocratic, remote leadership. But she had lived through the War and knew the value of European unity. For her, the efforts to unite Europe after 1945 were an extremely precious political gain. All attempts should be made to preserve peace and harmony in Europe. So the Queen would favour a model of close cooperation between nations, in a spirit of respect for the diversity and independence of each.

Tracy let her gaze linger on Buckingham Palace. Whatever the future holds, we have to safeguard this nation, she thought. She knew then who she would invite the next day to Chequers, her weekend residence, to discuss the situation discreetly. Formulating a plan of action, animated again now she had an idea of how to proceed, she went back along the Mall, as the soft drizzle continued to fall.

Chequers

The gentle hills of the Chilterns lie about forty miles to the north-west of London. Rising 876 feet at their highest, the Chilterns cover parts of Oxfordshire, Buckinghamshire, Hertfordshire and Bedfordshire, and form an idyllic hilly landscape of hedgerows, peaceful meadows dotted with white sheep, and woodlands where ash, oak and beech reign supreme. The woods are carpeted with bluebells in spring and turn golden brown in autumn, colouring the landscapes with their changing hues. Man has always exploited the resources of this beautiful area. The woods supplied the construction and furniture industries. The meadows provided cultivation and grazing. The chalky hills were the sites of quarries and have enabled a wine growing industry to exist since Roman times. Small towns steeped in history, adorable villages with stone churches, half-timbered houses and thatched roofs alongside old brick buildings with ochre tiles, are part of a rural charm that captivates tourists and walkers.

It is here, in the middle of a large estate, set far apart from any neighbours, that Chequers, the country residence of the British Prime Ministers, is located. Sightseeing is forbidden, and the house is somewhat mysterious to the general public.

The main entrance to the property, the grandest, along Victoria Drive, lined with beeches at the behest of Winston Churchill, is reserved for Prime Ministers and heads of state. Other guests enter by a less formal route, also through the grounds. Whichever way they approach the house, all visitors converge on the gravel sweep on the east side of the house. They drive round a raised lawn bed in the shape of a four leafed-clover, under the stony gaze of the goddess Hygeia. There they come upon a Tudor-style dwelling, dating mainly from the sixteenth century, built of brown and ochre brickwork. Large mullioned windows, several bays topped with gables, soften the austerity of a simple architecture. The frontage on the entrance courtyard does not immediately convey the true size of the house, whose rectangular shape was once arranged around a central courtyard (this space was largely covered over in the nineteenth century, to create the Great Hall), and whose north and south wings are the longest. The north wing, somewhat austere, overlooks a vast expanse of lawn. The south side of the house, more pleasant, is bordered by a terrace overlooking a flowerbed of box trees and roses. But what creates the real charm of the house, apart from the situation in lovely countryside, is the warm and comfortable interior. The Hawtrey Room, with its wood-panelled walls, and upholstered furniture arranged around a beautiful fireplace and in the nook of a bay window, welcomes guests as soon as they come from the hallway. Further in, in the middle of the former courtyard, the imposing Great Hall, richly furnished, two storeys high, lit by a wide mullioned bay, provides a beautiful reception room. A piano is there for guests to play. The delightful White Parlour, a former boudoir, with delicate eighteenth century furniture, such as a glass cabinet containing fine porcelain, is a haven of peace for the occupants, a lovely place to take tea. The comfortable bedrooms all have their own distinct style. Finally, the huge grounds allow plenty of walks through tree lined meadows. From the tops of the surrounding small hills a magnificent view of the area unfolds.

The fascinating history of Chequers had enthralled Tracy. In the sixteenth century William Hawtrey was a merchant, a founding member of the Muscovy Company of London, which had a monopoly on Anglo-Russian trade. His family had owned Chequers for many generations. Marrying a wealthy widow, Agnes Losse, William used the couple's joint fortune for extensive reconstruction and expansion. The works, completed in 1565, comprised most of what forms Chequers today.

It was then that the house entered English national history for the first time. William Hawtrey had barely finished his renovations when he received orders from the Privy Council to take Lady Mary Grey into his home. This potential heir to the throne was about twenty years old and being punished by Queen Elizabeth for an unapproved marriage. The elder sister of Lady Mary, Lady Jane Grey, had been proclaimed queen in 1553, under the dead king's will, in order to prevent the accession of the Catholic Mary, daughter of Henry VIII. In a reversal of fortunes, the Privy Council had annulled the will nine days later and proclaimed Mary Queen; Lady Jane was thrown in prison in the Tower of London and executed the following year, at the age of sixteen or seventeen. Her younger sister Lady Mary was therefore under intense scrutiny. She was locked in a room at Chequers for two years, before being assigned to another residence, probably to the relief of William Hawtrey.

About a century and a half later, John Russel, grandson of the Lord Protector of the Commonwealth of England, Scotland and Ireland, Oliver Cromwell, married Joanna Rivett, heiress of the property. Several portraits of Oliver Cromwell's family are now on display at Chequers, as well as the Parliamentary General's death mask.

In the Long Gallery, on the first floor of Chequers, there is also an oak pedestal table which was Napoleon's on St. Helena, some of the Emperor's military records, a few letters, his scarlet and gold dispatch case, and two pistols. The other side of the gallery houses medals and a watch belonging to his arch enemy, Admiral Nelson.

But the event that would really bring Chequers into British history was it being left to the government, in a document dated 1917, by the last owner of the house, Lord Lee of Fareham. After a career as a soldier and diplomat, Arthur Lee entered politics in 1900, becoming a Conservative MP for the constituency of Fareham. Renowned for his honesty and dynamism, Lord Lee did not have a personal fortune. While serving as a military attaché in Washington, he fell in love with Ruth Moore, daughter of the wealthy New York banker John Godfrey Moore. The couple were married on December 23rd, 1899, settling in England the following year. In 1909, looking for a pleasant country estate in the area, the Lees were won over by this mansion. They rented the estate and carried out extensive restoration work. When the opportunity to buy Chequers arose in 1917, Ruth and her sister Faith provided the money. They immediately transferred the property to Arthur, "in deepest gratitude and appreciation for the rare and remarkable qualities he has shown in his life from the two people who know him best and most intimately in the whole world". The Lees, however, had another project in mind: with no children of their own, they were considering giving up the property, at their death, to the British government to serve as a second home to the Prime Ministers of the country. Arthur Lee foresaw that twentieth-century leaders would come from all walks of life. Many would not have their own country estates to retreat to. A residence like Chequers "could [not] do anything but good...". The tranquillity of Chequers, its roots in history, its location in the heart of the countryside, would act as balancing factors, calming the most tempestuous politicians, bringing them the sense of historical continuity. As Arthur Lee wrote, "In the city-bred men especially, the periodic contact with the most typical rural life would create and preserve a just sense of proportion between the claims of town and country". The pure air of the Chilterns would have a beneficial effect and "the better the health of our rulers the more sanely they will rule". Lord Lee offered Chequers as a bequest to the nation. Lloyd George, head of the British government, accepted the plan with enthusiasm. Parliament approved the legacy in late 1917, with the Lees retaining the right to use Chequers until the end of their lives.

The house had already been made available to the nation as a military hospital between 1914 and 1916. In October 1917, at Lee's invitation, a meeting of the Allied Powers was held, at which General Foch was present, to discuss the principle of a single command of the troops. At his departure, Foch, aware of Lee's plans, wrote in the Visitors' Book: "England's affairs will run even more smoothly when her Prime Minister is housed at Chequers". After the Armistice, Arthur Lee decided to transfer the property during his lifetime. A final dinner was held on January 8th, 1921, bringing together Lloyd George, his wife, and several distinguished guests. Arthur Lee gave a farewell address at the end of the evening. Then, full of emotion, he and Ruth left the home they had occupied for twelve years and loved so much. Lee, Minister of Agriculture, also left his government post soon after. He did, however, continue to pursue an active public career and continued his philanthropy. In 1932, with funding from Samuel Courtauld, he founded the famous Courtauld Institute of Fine Arts at the University of London, to which he bequeathed a collection of artworks.

A stained-glass window at Chequers commemorates the Lees' gift: "This house of peace and ancient memories was given to England as a thank-offering for her deliverance in the Great War 1914-18 and as a place of rest and recreation for her Prime Ministers for ever." Above this inscription, the initials A for Arthur and R for Ruth, intertwined, testify to the couple's love. They echo the W and A, the initials of William and Agnes Hawtrey, found on the north facade of the house.

Almost every Prime Minister since Lloyd George has enjoyed the comfort of Chequers. Winston Churchill spent long periods there during the war, recording several of his radio broadcasts in the Hawtrey Room. Margaret Thatcher made references to the estate in her memoirs. She and her husband liked it so much that Denis Thatcher said "Chequers is the reason you become Prime Minister".

* * *

It was in this house, so rich in history, that Tracy, like her predecessors, spent most of her weekends. As a walker, and not having her own country house, Chequers was a paradise, far from the frenetic activity of Downing Street.

She rarely had any leisure time, however. A Prime Minister's weekends are still busy with work and meetings. On the last Saturday of January, arriving from London at 10 in the morning, she immediately started work on her files, needing to take care of several matters before receiving Laura Soriens for lunch. In the Hawtrey Room, where a pleasant fire was burning, she annotated the papers she had brought with her, noting in a few brief words her opinion or her instructions.

She had invited Laura Soriens rather than the Chairman of the HGB bank. Although she had known the latter for years, she was suspicious of his advice because he always had hidden plans in his own interest. She would not have that risk with the Chief Executive, who would tell the Prime Minister her thoughts without prevarication. This is what she needed most today: that the people she talked with speak to her frankly, even if they should express an opinion different to hers. She knew that her two guests that day were not in favour of Brexit XXL. She would give them a chance to express their opinions freely. Chequers provided a discreet, ideal setting for this type of discussion.

Soriens arrived at 12.30. Tracy received her in the Great Hall and, while waiting for lunch, showed her a series of pictures of famous visitors to Chequers. The two women then went into the dining room. Tracy started the discussion very bluntly. She wanted to know how badly HGB would be affected by Construct's bankruptcy.

"On the purely financial side, it will be a significant loss for us, but we can absorb it," said the Chief Executive. "The bank has been experiencing difficulties in its British operations, but our operations abroad are profitable. What we're afraid of in the Construct case is not the actual direct loss, it's the ripple effect. Construct's bankruptcy, after so many years of economic difficulties, is the last straw. If it had occurred in a healthy market, it would have been manageable. But in this nervous market, it may trigger a panic. Financial markets will plummet, just because in these circumstances there will be many more sellers than buyers. We should therefore expect a significant stock market shock. Some of Construct's suppliers will also go bankrupt. Investors who have paid for developments in advance will find themselves in trouble. Bank customers, worried about their solvency, will want to withdraw their money. The pound will come under heavy attack by speculators. Construct's bankruptcy will generate a chain reaction."

"I understand all of that," said Tracy with an anxious tone in her voice, however. "What do you think the government can do to prevent a crisis next week?"

"I'm afraid it's too late," replied Soriens frankly. "Certainly, the government can do some things to reduce the scale of the crisis, such as reminding the public that bank deposits are guaranteed up to a certain amount. The Bank of England will also take the appropriate technical measures, by intervening in the markets. But investors will all want the same thing: to take their money out of the system, sell their shares, maybe buy foreign currency and invest abroad before it's too late. People no longer believe in the economy's ability to reboot; Construct failing is a spectacular example of that. Technical measures will not be enough against that kind of trend."

"I am going to ask you a direct question, Mrs Soriens, and I would like you to answer it with your usual frankness. Do you think that the country should change its economic orientation and in particular its position vis-à-vis the European Union?"

"Prime Minister, since we are at Chequers, a house steeped in history, allow me to reply by quoting your most illustrious predecessor, Winston Churchill: 'If Europe were once united in the sharing of its common inheritance, there would be no limit to the happiness, to the prosperity and glory which its three or four hundred million people would enjoy... We must build a kind of United States of Europe... The first step is to form a Council of Europe'."

"The same Churchill said that 'Every time we have to decide between Europe and the open sea, it is always the open sea we shall choose'," Tracy said with a smile.

"We must keep our sovereignty, but we can't survive without access to the European market. We have to negotiate our return, Prime Minister. Our industry and our financial sector can't progress in the UK market alone."

Lunch continued along those lines. Tracy appreciated her guest's direct answers. She asked her a number of technical questions about the measures to be taken in the short term. She also defended her vision of a successful Brexit. But she could not muster her usual conviction. Today she felt all too keenly the limits of the principles she had built up over the past five years. After lunch, she suggested to her guest that they take a short walk. The rain that had fallen the day before had stopped; there was a cloudy sky, cold but with a few rays of sunshine. The two women, walking fast to warm up, took quite a long route through the grounds. They discussed the economy but also chatted about this and that. At about four o'clock Tracy thanked her departing guest.

"Your views have been helpful," she told her. "I can't implement what you have suggested straight away. But I will think about it."

Laura Soriens refrained from insisting. She felt that her convictions had not left her hostess indifferent. One of these days, perhaps, the Prime Minister would announce a new policy.

After the Chief Executive's departure, Tracy strolled briefly in the south garden. She admired how well-kept it was, despite the winter, which left her no flowers. The box hedge was trimmed, the gravel paths perfectly raked, the lawn impeccably green. She nearly stepped on a snail on the path, picked it up and put it in the grass. "We have to get through the winter," she thought. "Spring will come for the country as surely it will for this garden." On this optimistic thought, she returned to the sitting room to finish her paperwork.

John Klin was expected at Chequers for six thirty that evening. No expectation could be less certain, however. A respected professor with recognised expertise and holder of the Chair of Political Economy at the London School of Economics, Klin was also very absent-minded. He could make an appointment with you for six o'clock today and arrive the following day at six o'clock. The first time Tracy had invited him to Chequers, he had turned up...at Windsor Castle, convinced he had been invited there by the Queen. He had explained to the bemused guards that the Queen had asked him to come to lunch to explain his views on the country's economy. Having received from the butler the very definite confirmation that he was not on the day's guest list, and not being allowed to send a message to the sovereign to inform her of his presence, Klin had left in his little Fiat, complaining about the Queen making invitations without informing her staff. Meanwhile, Tracy, anxious about the non-arrival of her guest, had asked the police if there had been an accident. The anecdote had been all over the tabloids the next day and given the readers a good laugh. When the Queen was informed, she sent an official invitation to Klin the following week for a luncheon at Windsor, playfully adding that her butler had been made aware.

Today, however, John Klin was driving over in his Fiat. His wife had reminded him of the time of the appointment and the route to Chequers. He arrived at exactly six thirty, which made Tracy think that indeed things had certainly changed in the kingdom of Great Britain.

The Professor was invited to have an aperitif in the White Parlour. Having followed events at Construct closely over the last few months, he was aware of the latest developments. The conversation turned quickly to the consequences for the economy. Klin was very conversant with the national statistics. He showed that Construct's bankruptcy was likely to be followed by many others. He conceded to Tracy that some sectors of the economy were doing well, but said that overall, the country was in a very bad state and was on the brink of a major crisis. He said he had several graphs proving it but realised he had left his folder at home, which made the Prime Minister smile. Klin got onto criticism of the geopolitical implications of Brexit.

"British policy has always been to intervene on the continent to keep the European balance. We've often been with the

Germans against the French, or with the French against the Germans, because one or other of the two was becoming too powerful. Brexit takes away the possibility of intervening in European matters. Even worse, we've managed to engineer a situation where Germany and France are allied against the UK. The principles of diplomacy in the past still hold for the modern economic system: we need balance of trade on a European scale. The imbalance in the system has been to our detriment."

The Prime Minister reminded him of the many reforms undertaken by her government, including the relaxation of employment laws and the simplification of procedures, which increased the country's competitiveness and should lead to benefits. John Klin's answer was that it was like oiling the door hinges while the house was on fire. The country's economy was suffocating; it was crucial to get it breathing again by fully regaining access to the European market.

"We no longer have the luxury of time," he explained. "What was still possible two or three years ago is not possible today; it is critical to understand this. Our companies, our individual investors, our banks, were still able to withstand shocks. But this capacity has been greatly eroded. The Bank of England can't inject the same sums as before into the markets. The government's own credit is beginning to be questioned and the rating agencies are considering downgrading Britain's rating. A significant shock like the collapse of Construct may be enough to tip the balance."

"Do you have any good news for me?" Tracy forced a smile.

"None, unfortunately, but please consider the following: if, next week or in the near future, you were to announce the opening of negotiations to return to the European Economic Area, you would see the markets and public confidence bounce back instantly. If on the other hand you announce a continuation of the policy of Brexit XXL, both will collapse. Isn't that a clear answer on the choice you need to make?"

"You know the political constraints of this choice, Mr Klin. A large part of the electorate is not ready to accept all the conditions necessary to access the European Economic Area, such as the free movement of persons or the contribution to the European budget, for example. I don't see how the government could take that position in these circumstances."

"The country is in danger, madam. You have to tell them the truth."

Tracy did not blame Klin for his plain speaking. She had asked him for his frank opinion, and she listened to his advice. She liked his direct style and passion. And moreover, all the economic experts she'd seen since yesterday had come up with the same analysis. Without a change of direction, the country was on the verge of a major crisis.

As they had covered most of the arguments, the conversation turned to other subjects. Towards ten o'clock in the evening, the Professor left, not without having had to look for his car keys for a good quarter of an hour. It was Tracy who had finally found them, in a flowerpot in the hall.

As she came back into the living room, amused, she received a call on her mobile. It was Guy Wick, one of the most influential members of the Conservative party and fervent defender of Brexit XXL.

"We have noted that you are consulting a lot of anti-Brexit people," he told her bluntly. "Don't think of following their advice. You know that the party would not support you." His tone was cold, almost threatening.

Tracy replied that she did not need lessons in how to run a government and that she would do what she had to do.

"Our country has chosen a course, we're not ones for changing at the first gust of wind," continued Guy Wick. "Your government will fall apart at the slightest sign of weakness. And we can bring you down."

Tracy told him to go to hell and ended the call. She did not want to have that conversation at this time of night. But she knew she could not ignore the views of his wing of the party.

She went up to bed. She had cleared her diary the day after of all appointments. She wanted a Sunday dedicated to rest and reflection, to prepare for the ordeals of the coming week.

The crisis of February 2022

The collapse of Construct was announced on Monday, January 31st, around 10 am, after the Extraordinary Meeting of the Board of Directors. Rumours had been swirling around all weekend and the official statement did not come as a surprise to the financial community.

At opening, the stock markets reacted very negatively, particularly driven by banks and property companies. The pound plummeted. The Cabinet met in the morning and several technical measures were announced at the end of the meeting. Tracy Meller, however, did not make a public announcement, as her speech was planned for the following day. She spent the day consulting with political leaders, both from her own party and from the Opposition. The Chancellor of the Exchequer, invited on to the BBC, gave a reassuring speech: Construct was bad news, but the British economy was strong enough to overcome it. Banks, in particular, were prepared to withstand shocks of this magnitude. There had been no lack of supervision by the government. The Chancellor avoided answering any questions about changing the economic policy and stuck to purely technical answers. What he did not say was that intense discussions had been taking place since Friday between London and the European Commission, very discreetly, to speed up the management of the so-called transitional provisions: it was a matter of extending the provisions that had been negotiated in 2018 for four years, beyond 2022. The government was counting on the announcement of these talks by the Prime Minister to create a positive effect on public opinion, as the imminent expiry of the temporary measures was generating additional concerns. Tracy had delayed her public announcement to Tuesday, February 1st, so as to allow time for the parties to agree on a joint statement. A precise schedule of negotiations would be announced, as well as the list of topics that would be dealt with.

The news of the secret talks filtered out in financial circles late on Monday afternoon. That was enough to reverse the downward trend in the markets, which gained back some of the losses of the earlier part of the day. The pound also began to recover. The rumours grew after the markets closed, and it was even whispered that the next day Mrs Meller would be announcing not only the start of discussions on the transitional provisions, but even a more general framework of negotiations for a possible return of the country to the European Economic Area. This rumour came from an interpretation of the meetings she had had in recent days and in particular on Saturday at Chequers, which had filtered through to the newspapers: if she were having meetings with Laura Soriens and John Klin, whose anti-Brexit opinions were well known, it meant that she was planning something. Most financial players took market positions on a sharp rise for the next day, counting on a spectacular recovery of markets after the Prime Minister's speech. It was a unique opportunity to make profits to compensate for the losses suffered since the January crisis. Late Monday afternoon, Tracy spoke on the phone to the President of the European Commission, which intensified speculation.

Worried by the turn of events, several Conservative ministers and party members contacted the Prime Minister in the early evening. They reminded her, in more polite tones than Guy Wick's, but no less firmly, of their formal opposition to any movement towards a return to the European Economic Area.

On Tuesday, February 1st, Tracy unexpectedly postponed her speech until the end of the afternoon. She spent the morning in further talks with several of her Ministers. Now all sorts of rumours were going round about the statement she was going to make.

A number of journalists explained that Mrs Meller, in a major political coup, was going to announce a Cabinet reshuffle and a start to negotiations for membership of the European Economic Area or the European Free Trade Area. They considered her pragmatic enough to abandon a policy that did not work and thought that she could find a majority in Parliament to support this position. They added that this was the only way to avoid Scotland demanding independence and that the Prime Minister would prioritise national unity.

Other journalists, on the contrary, thought that Meller would resign after major disagreements with her party. According to them, she had been on borrowed time since January, with the crisis having shown the failure of her management. The Conservative Party was nervous about polls showing gains for Labour. Several party members advocated a change of Prime Minister before the elections, which were to be held no later than May 2023. These members, led by Guy Wick, suspected Meller of having lost faith in the hard Brexit that she and the party had been championing since 2018, which was a capital crime in their eyes. They remembered that Meller had spent the first eighteen months of her term trying to negotiate with the European Union and had only embarked on Brexit XXL after the failure of these discussions. That made it look like she had jumped on the bandwagon at the last moment, and what's worse, had now begun to associate with anti-Brexit figures.

The most daring journalists were betting on a coalition government, justified by the dire straits the country was in, with the Labour leader, Jeremy Jones, in a key position, such as Foreign Secretary or Chancellor. Jones had spent more than two hours on Monday alone with the Prime Minister and was refusing to comment.

A very few reporters thought that Meller would only announce some technical measures and offer nothing new, just the continuation of her policy. Their analysis was based on the premise that the Prime Minister could not scrap the policy that she had been pursuing for four years and would not take the risk of a break with the hard-line wing of her party, fifteen months before the next election. She would confine herself to a few announcements on the temporary provisions expiring over the course of the year and would promise a recovery of the economy before 2023.

The biggest flights of fancy came from those who thought that Meller would announce nothing less than a new referendum on Brexit, an idea she had rejected every time the question was asked during her term.

Investors were also divided. Many had already spent a difficult morning trying to unravel the speculative positions they had taken the previous day in expectation of today. The Prime Minister's speech was now planned for five o'clock, so they were having to reposition themselves for Wednesday. Many lost significant sums. The problem was that the postponement of Meller's speech had raised more questions than answers. Given the extent of the rumours, the financiers did not know how to approach the market. Some, most in fact, speculated on a rise, others on a fall; a minority preferred to wait. Nerves were jangling, though, and the markets spent the day swinging back and forth.

At 4:50 pm, a lectern was put up in front of 10 Downing Street. The press, tired from hours of waiting in the cold, hurried to their reserved area. At 5 pm, Tracy came out. She made an effort to smile but her face was tense. Dressed in a dark blue suit and a warm white coat, she put on her glasses and began her speech.

"The bankruptcy of such a prestigious and important establishment as Construct is news that concerns us all. Since last Friday, when the company's management informed us of the situation, the government has worked tirelessly to identify the most appropriate measures to respond to this crisis. An action committee has been set up, at my request, by the Chancellor of the Exchequer, who will take steps to protect the employees of the company, as best we can, by supporting them through training and redeployment programmes. Measures will also be taken to expedite compensation of individual creditors through the sale of the company's available assets. The Chancellor will communicate the full details of these measures tomorrow. We are wholeheartedly with the victims of this event and will do everything possible to mitigate the wider effects.

"I would like to point out that although this bankruptcy is serious for the people concerned, our economy, worth in excess of 1900 billion pounds, is well able to absorb shocks of this magnitude. Credit institutions have sufficient resources to deal with default risks. Our banks are strong.

"I have heard a lot of comments in recent days calling for backtracking on our Brexit policy because of the current economic difficulties. If we followed those recommendations, we would have to go back on everything that we have been putting in place for the last four years. Above all, we would not be respecting the will of British citizens, who confirmed their intentions with two votes. Our country has chosen the path of independence, that is the will of the people, and the government must action it. Over the coming months we will continue the gradual transformation of our economy to this end. Certainly there are, and there will continue to be, difficulties. But our country is on a path of reform that will ensure tomorrow's prosperity, and we will continue in that direction."

Adding a few words to rally her fellow citizens to show solidarity in these difficult times, Tracy took her leave and returned to her office.

The journalists were stunned by the Prime Minister's speech. Not an inch of change. Not a word about the transitional provisions. Construct's bankruptcy treated as a mere technicality. But it was the financial industries that were most affected. In TV interviews, their most well-known personalities expressed their consternation. Continuing the same policy looked to them like economic suicide. Were the Prime Minister and her party so blind? The traders urgently placed orders for the next day, now trying to unravel the positions they had taken earlier. All those who had bet on the markets rising were risking big losses. US markets, where it was still early in the day, prepared for massive sales. It was the perfect storm for a panic. James Callagher, Chairman of HGB Bank, rang his associate Luke to give him the starting signal for his plan of attack.

★ ★ ★

The next day, Wednesday, February 2nd, 2022, the stock market opened sharply down, heralding one of the worst days of the London Stock Exchange, which would be remembered as Black Wednesday. At noon the main index had lost twelve percent. Trading was suspended for thirty minutes. Stock value in the billions of pounds went up in smoke. Confusion was rife.

Never, perhaps, had a Prime Minister's speech been followed by such catastrophic effects. The Bank of England, under the leadership of Denniel, intervened in the markets, announcing that it was ready to take all necessary measures to prevent a complete breakdown of the financial system. The government made several technical announcements. But nothing helped. Investors had pinned all their hopes on a change of policy. Let down, they had lost all confidence. The shares hit downward resistance thresholds that they had not come anywhere near in the past five years and crossed those points of no return.

During Prime Minister's Question Time, the Labour leader issued a virulent indictment of the government's negligence and the reckless way, according to him, in which the Prime Minister was managing the crisis. He called again for urgent elections to take place. Tracy replied that the foundations of the national economy remained healthy and that the collapse of the markets was unwarranted and an overreaction. Acrimonious exchanges followed between the parties, which got so bad that the Speaker had to suspend the sitting.

When the markets closed at four thirty, the FTSE 100 had fallen by fourteen percent, a catastrophic performance. The pound had fallen by five per cent, partly bolstered by Bank of England interventions. Analysts now feared a stock market collapse in the coming weeks similar to that of 2008-2009, which would lead to widespread bankruptcies. The consequences would be worse, because the government no longer had the means to intervene to any significant extent.

Around 5 pm, the rating agency Standard & Poor's published a press release announcing the downgrading of the British national rating to BBB+, an unthinkable ranking for a government that, just before Brexit, was still rated AAA. The news came after the Stock Exchange closed and was to have a disastrous effect the next day.

* * *

At the same time, Guy Wick made a statement to the press, emphasising his full approval of the Prime Minister's speech. He said that a return to the European Economic Area would be a sleight of hand solution, which would throw the United Kingdom back into an economic dependence on Europe. According to him, Britain had a global destiny, it had to forge its own economic agreements with all nations and free itself from disproportionate reliance on European countries. Moreover, as the modern economy revolved around global trade, privileging a specific geographical area made no sense. Even if the transition was painful, it had to be seen through. He accused the financial markets of speculation, which was harming the country's interests. He hinted, however, that the government could have done more to improve the economic situation. In fact, Wick was preparing the ground for a leadership bid, and to become Prime Minister himself. He had bet on both sides. If Meller changed course, he would attack her within the party, and take her down, because he still had enough members on his side. If she continued her policy, he would support her political line, but all the while hinting that the promised results were taking too long to come through, and that a change of leader had become necessary. His phone call to Chequers the previous Saturday was not intended to send a warning to Tracy Meller, as she had thought, but to sound out her position. Now that the Prime Minister had confirmed she was continuing on the Brexit route, Wick was putting the first steps of his plan into action. He had to be careful not to go too fast: he had to be party leader by the end of the year, at the time of the Party Conference, to be able to present himself as a saviour before the elections, but without having to take responsibility for the country's economic woes, as he would have just taken office.

In truth, Guy Wick was surprised by the Prime Minister's speech. He had thought that Tracy Meller, convinced by figures like Laura Soriens and John Klin, and desperately tired of the economic difficulties, had decided to abandon the Brexit XXL ideology. The abrupt way she had answered when he rang her at Chequers had reinforced his conviction. He had spent Monday preparing the ground for a revolt with several party dignitaries. Tuesday's speech caught him off guard. He wondered if he had misjudged the situation, or whether the Prime Minister had changed her mind at the last moment, for some unknown reason.

Nobody, except Tracy, could answer that question. Although she had spoken to a lot of people on Monday 31st and Tuesday 1st, she had not revealed her true intentions to those she met with, even to her Ministers, in keeping with her usual habit of making the final decisions alone. The reality was that her choice was made on Monday evening. Thinking long and hard about the situation on her Sunday spent alone at Chequers, she came to believe that Britain was facing a significant financial crisis in the near future. The data she had been receiving from her departments and the Chancellor of the Exchequer for several days were clear on this point. Her recent conversations with the Governor of the Bank of England, with Laura Soriens and John Klin, only served to confirm her analysis. She had also concluded, painfully but clear-sightedly, that the hard Brexit line she had implemented since 2018 was no longer economically viable. However, as an experienced head of government, she knew that she could only make a radical change if the political conditions were right. Now, her analysis was that the present circumstances would not permit change. Her political talks on Monday corroborated this belief. First of all, a significant segment of the Conservative party, as Wick demonstrated, remained fundamentally opposed to any relaxation of Brexit.

This opposition, almost ideological, often virulent, would have triggered a crisis within the party in the event of her changing direction. The Conservative party would probably have split. In these circumstances, it would be impossible for her to obtain a majority in Parliament. The number of Conservative MPs who would support the new line was not insignificant, but not decisive. An alliance with the Labour Party could not be countenanced. The opposition party, favourable to Europe, was trying to bring about a General Election, which it was sure to win, so it had no interest in supporting a Conservative Prime Minister in trouble.

On the other hand, the country itself was not ready. While more and more people, according to the polls, wanted a return to the European common market, that desire was usually accompanied by requirements for national sovereignty that were not compatible with European demands. The first stumbling block was the freedom of movement of people, which remained a sensitive subject, even among those who were in favour of Europe. A significant proportion of the population, like the Conservative party, remained fundamentally opposed to any idea of return. Reopening the subject would be perceived by those people, most of whom voted for her in 2018, as a real betrayal. Tracy had campaigned on the successful implementation of a hard line Brexit. A policy U-turn would not have been understood or accepted by those voters and would have once again highlighted the deep lines of division splitting British society.

Lastly, Europe itself was not ready for further discussion. That had been confirmed to her during her long discussions with the President of the European Commission. The Continent had its own difficulties, with several Eurozone countries having worrying levels of debt, which needed a lot of internal negotiations to clean up. Some countries, including France, were in an election year; Meller did not particularly want to relive the situation of 2017, where an entire year had been lost. The President of the Commission also stressed the risk of an extreme party taking power in France. Talks with Britain would fuel the fire before the elections and could become obsolete if one of the extreme parties was elected. The president had therefore advocated waiting until the end of the year.

Facing the unenviable prospect of a major financial crisis without being able to implement a solution, Tracy had decided on the only course of action that corresponded to her life-long political convictions: face the difficulties square on, rely on the extraordinary resources of the country she loved so much, and leave it in the hands of fate, waiting for better days. The worst case was not necessarily a given, the economic crisis might be less dramatic than the experts were forecasting, but even if it was, the country would still come through it. She had certainly not considered resigning: she would not leave her post while the country was in turmoil. Nor would she call an election, because in the current political climate, it would have caused serious divisions.

Since the country had to stay the course, she certainly would not give the impression of doing it reluctantly or under duress. She decided to demonstrate to the country that she was totally resolute and ready to lead the nation in the further difficulties it was going through. She moved her speech to the afternoon to have time to prepare it along those lines. However, her assessment of two important factors was flawed. The first was the expectations of the financial markets. Investors and bankers had been relentlessly advocating a return to Europe for months or even years. For them, the economic situation was now such that there was no other possible solution. Since the January crisis they had pinned their hopes on Tracy Meller making a change, as they knew her to be pragmatic and genuinely concerned for the good of the country, and it was believed that she was having doubts. Her speech was a grave disappointment and robbed them of any hope of obtaining a new policy. From then on, they had only one possible approach: to sell as soon as possible, and save what they could, before a worse collapse.

The other factor Tracy did not take into account was the extent of the economic crisis that threatened the country. She may have been aware that a financial explosion would be likely, with markets fluctuating wildly, but she had no idea of the scale or duration that this would involve. The shock of Wednesday, February 2nd hit her very hard. She thought it was artificial, swelled by a momentary panic or reckless speculation. The future would prove to her that it was not a temporary crisis, but an economic earthquake even more brutal than what the country had experienced during the great financial crisis of 2008-2009. It was the British economy, in one fell swoop, adjusting to the long-term reality of Brexit XXL. The difficulties experienced since the 2016 vote had led to a drop in purchasing power, a fall in the value of the currency, and unemployment, as well as relocation and restructuring. These changes had been gradual, mitigated by the wealth accumulated by Britain during so many years of growth before Brexit. And hard as they had been, especially in certain sectors such as industry and banks, these developments had happened bit by bit, like the coming of winter and a gradual acclimatisation to the cold. People did not fully appreciate the general weakening of the economy, especially since the success of some sectors led them to believe that a transition was taking place. Construct's bankruptcy was a painful wake up call. In real terms, it should not have been an insurmountable threat, far from it. However, it was not only a shockwave triggering the collapse of levels of the economy that had held out up till then, but also a revelation of the collective reaction of a nation which suddenly found itself face to face with the inevitable consequences of a process of change that no one could control any more.

The crisis spreads

Nick Walderg was a twenty-five year old trader at HGB Bank. On the evening of Wednesday, February 2nd, he went home exhausted from his crazy day. Home at his flat, he had a row with his girlfriend, Nancy, because she was insisting that they spend the weekend with friends in Oxford, while he was planning to rest and do nothing at all after this already exhausting week. They argued for twenty minutes, neither giving way. Then, when Nancy asked him to take a day off on Friday, Nick got angry, told her that she didn't understand anything about his work, and went out, slamming the door behind him.

At the pub down the street, Nick ordered a pint. He saw his friend Mark Tweeds, a financial analyst in the competing bank, Standards. They got talking straight away about the day's events.

"It's panic at Standards," said Mark. "There will be no buyers in the markets over the next few weeks; prices are going to carry on collapsing. I spent my whole day doing calculations – the country's going to plunge into a recession worse than anything we've had before."

"I was battling to save my portfolio all day," Nick replied. "It was sheer madness. Prices dropped by several hundred points in a few minutes, went up, then went down again even further. The systems were freaking out and so were the people. I managed to sell some stocks early on, but overall I'm well into the red, and tomorrow will be even worse, with the downgrade."

"I just don't understand Meller," Mark said. "Construct going bust offered her a perfect opportunity to change her policy. She didn't seize the moment. Does the government really not get it? Don't they look at the data?"

"They're only thinking about the political repercussions," said Nick. "If she changed policy, Wick would bring her down. She just wanted to keep her job. She wants to see out her five years and then step down. She doesn't realise that in the meantime the country is going under."

"All the same, there should be a minimum qualification in economics to become Prime Minister. If they all understood the figures better, they wouldn't do these idiotic things. What are you going to do tomorrow?"

"I don't know. If it drops another ten percent, I'm dead. Besides, they're already talking about layoffs at the bank. In just one day HGB lost a billion pounds! Maybe I won't have a job by the end of the week – who knows? At least then I'll be able to go off on a long weekend with Nancy!" he added mournfully.

"Oh, hadn't you planned to spend the evening with her?"

"Yes, but we had a row. About the weekend in fact. It's my fault; I came home with my nerves in tatters."

The two young men looked around. The pub was full. A lot of people had come in for a drink after work before heading home. Nick noticed cheerful conversations, people were laughing and seemed relaxed. But as he listened more carefully, he heard that most of the conversations revolved around the crisis. The laughter helped to let off steam and put the day's harsh realities aside for a moment. In this rather expensive part of London, a lot of residents worked in financial institutions. Nick wondered how many other people in the pub were worried about losing their jobs in the weeks to come.

"You should go back home to Nancy," Mark told him. "Don't stay out with an argument between you."

"Not now," Nick replied. "I'm still too tense, I might just blow up again. She doesn't understand that I need to devote all my energy to my work these days."

"I think she's trying to protect you. There hasn't really been a quiet day in months. She doesn't want this job to take over your whole life."

"It's true that it's been non-stop madness, especially since the January crisis. That's why we were all expecting a real change, to finally put an end to this disaster. They really are sods, this government."

"Look, there's Luke Trosden."

"I wonder how he did today."

Luke Trosden was a legend among traders. He had managed to make a lot of money during the 2008-2009 crisis, by playing the markets successfully. He had reinvested when stocks were at their lowest in 2009 and amassed a fortune he had managed and increased until 2015. Since the Brexit vote, he had been dispensing advice in the financial papers and on television. He claimed to have doubled his assets since 2016, while markets were doing no favours. Nobody knew if it was true or what his strategy had been.

"He doesn't look too happy," Nick said. "Maybe his portfolio took a hit ..."

Luke Trosden, who knew Mark, came over to shake their hands.

"Tough day..." said Mark.

"I've sold everything," said Luke. "The whole lot. I'm just moving my last funds abroad. I lost ten percent, but at least I'm safe. Luckily, I've been cashing in for several years, which has taken the edge off. I'm out of this madhouse. I'm going to Canada next week. You should get out too, mate. You're young, go to Europe, America, wherever you want, but don't waste your time sticking around here."

On this astonishing note, Luke headed off to shake other hands. He was advising everyone to leave.

"Unbelievable," said Mark. "Luke Trosden leaving the City?"

"It's a very bad sign. Maybe he read the markets wrong. Or maybe he's pulling a fast one, he actually wants the markets to collapse so he can buy back at the lowest point, like in 2009. But that's still not good news."

"This crisis is doing me no good at all," continued Mark. "I was planning to finally buy a flat, with my end of February bonus to get me up to the purchase price. Now it looks like there's a real possibility we might get nothing this year."

"Hang on a bit," Nick told him. "If the property market collapses, you'll soon be able to buy a six-bedroom flat in Kensington Palace Gardens!"

The two friends burst out laughing. Kensington Palace Gardens, nicknamed "Billionaires' Row" was still one of the most expensive addresses in London. Even with a sharp drop in prices, it would be out of reach for Mark.

"Apparently that's where your bossman, the Chairman of HGB lives?"

"Yes, he's really loaded. This crisis is not going to bother him much."

"And Mrs Soriens?"

"She's not that rich. I mean, she gets a CEO's salary, I'm not worrying about her making ends meet. But she's not a multibillionaire. If the bank goes bankrupt, she'll have a problem, like the rest of us."

"Do you really think HGB will go under?" Mark asked, flabbergasted.

"If it carries on like this week, I don't know how HGB will get through it. Or the other banks for that matter."

"But that's impossible – the government will do something," Mark began, before breaking off and then saying "...unless they do nothing, like this week. We are really in deep. I'd give my right arm for a chat with Mrs Meller, and to give her a piece of my mind."

"You know what?" Nick said to him. "We can't let this eat us alive like this; there must be a solution. A country like ours, it's just not on to let it fall apart. In any case, I'm not leaving. Even if they fire me, I'll find work, anything. But I will not let my country down."

Nick got up and went to see Luke Trosden.

"I'm staying," he shouted. "I'm not going to leave this country. Whatever happens!" Luke Trosden looked at him and shrugged.

"Do what you want, mate. I'm off."

Nick came back to see Mark, who had watched the conversation without moving. "I'm going to see Nancy," he told him. "See you later!"

"See you," Mark replied, wondering what state his friend would be in next time he saw him.

Nick went back to the flat, kissed Nancy passionately and apologised.

Nancy replied that she was sorry too, that she shouldn't have insisted about the weekend. The two decided to finish the evening in a trendy club in town. Good music and a great atmosphere, that would help them forget this rotten day.

On their way to the Tube, Nancy said to Nick: "You didn't even ask me how my day went."

Nick smiled. "Well, I'm sorry – again. So: how was your day?"

Nancy laughed and told him that she had got a pay rise. The pharmaceutical company she worked for was doing good business and had been putting salaries up. How ironic in the middle of this crisis! Nick was amazed at the diversity of positions, between the banks and financial markets taking a dive, and the sectors that were thriving despite everything.

They got out of the Tube at Piccadilly Circus, went up Regent Street and turned down Vigo Street. They were heading for Centre, a popular London nightclub. Once he was in, Nick was caught up in the atmosphere which made him forget all his difficulties. No visitor to the club would have suspected that a major crisis was going on across the country. The place was crowded; hundreds of young people were dancing to the hits. Nick felt the rhythms that he loved. British pop music had dominated the world since the 1960s, but Brexit had given it a new lease of life, though no one was quite sure why. Had the crisis unleashed creative energies, had it increased the demand for music by customers eager to forget their troubles? One thing that was certain was that music producers had benefited greatly from the devaluation, which had increased their revenues from abroad. They had spotted talented new successors to The Beatles, The Rolling Stones, Genesis, Eric Clapton, The Police, Elton John, and so many others. British music was more innovative than ever and its heart was here in London, especially at this club aptly known as Centre.

The old hits were still popular though. Around midnight, the DJ started playing classic anthems from the 90s and 2000s, skilfully lifting the mood on the dance floor. When he put on Coldplay's "A Sky Full of Stars," the club went into a trance, somehow on the same frequency as that hit, released in 2014, when London was doing so well, when everything seemed possible for the capital, two years after the Olympics and two years before Brexit. The collective unconscious was deeply rooted in the memory of that golden age of London and aspired to recreate it. Like Nick, young Britons were not about to abandon their country, but on the contrary wanted to regenerate it. Nick danced with Nancy and knew that his future was here, in Britain.

★ ★ ★

The next day, Thursday, February 3rd, 2022, was as difficult as the day before for the markets. Standard and Poor's' decision to downgrade fuelled panic. A downgrading of the country's rating meant that lending money to Britain had become riskier than before. Now, any new government borrowing would have to be negotiated at a higher rate. This was the end for Philip Denniel's zero rates. The markets anticipated that this increase in the cost of the country's debt would weigh very heavily on the public finances, which were already in bad shape. The national debt, which had risen sharply since 2016, reaching more than 110% of GDP, would grow even faster. The country's financial margins for manoeuvre would be reduced and the risk of default became real. Stocks plunged 10% during the day, and 5% on Friday, a drop of more than 25% in three days, a disaster that ruined many investors.

Nick did not lose his job at the end of the week, but he knew his bank was struggling. Laura Soriens met with her executive committee every day to make very urgent decisions.

Tracy, meanwhile, spent these days under considerable pressure. She confronted the problems calmly, spending hours with the Chancellor of the Exchequer and her advisers, taking what technical measures they could to alleviate the impact of the crisis as much as possible. She had no free time, staying all weekend working at Downing Street. There would be no walks, no stay at Chequers to recharge.

She needed all her strength, however. Over the next two weeks, there was extreme volatility in the markets. There were some positive days as investors began to buy, thinking stocks had bottomed out. Then those days were followed by new drops, with no one knowing where it was going to stop. On February 14th, a small local bank, Merlin Bank, declared itself insolvent. The government, prompted by Tracy, encouraged by Philip Denniel, proceeded immediately to a capital increase with public funds. However, small depositors panicked and began to withdraw their money from all the banks. The banks had to impose a withdrawal limit to avoid a collapse of the entire banking system. The public, unable to access their cash, reduced their spending, which increased the crisis.

On the following Thursday, two weeks and one day after the start of the financial crisis, the first major demonstration took place in central London. The demonstrators, meeting in Hyde Park, came to express their unhappiness with the economic situation. A lot of the banners were calling for the government to resign. This demo was the first of a long series that would mark the year 2022.

The Democratic Alliance

As President Marquet was making a fuss of his dog, a golden retriever, in his office, one of his staff was shown in. He had brought the latest polls.

"Mr President, the two extreme parties are predicted to win in the first round of the presidential election, however we look at the figures. Their candidates are each forecast between 23 and 25% of the votes. We only have 20 to 22%."

"Don't people realise that these parties are just spinning a line?"

"No, Mr President. For them, all politicians are liars, including us. Now the other parties have failed, they're gravitating towards the ones offering a new alternative."

"I won't let it happen. I will not leave my country in the hands of adventurers, who will make unilateral decisions whose consequences will carry on affecting the nation for generations. It would be a disaster for France and spell the end for Europe. The human and economic impacts would be catastrophic."

"What are you going to do, Mr President?"

Marquet did not answer. He had a plan, an idea he had been mulling over for a few weeks, but it was still too early to reveal it.

"Let's go on TV," he said at last. "Continue the campaign, keep putting across our arguments. Try not to worry about the other parties. Focus all our attacks on the National Party and the Democratic Revolution Party. We need to push them to their limits."

"Very good, Mr President."

A few weeks later, on February 21st, after discreet negotiations, the President announced the formation of an electoral alliance between his party and two other moderate parties, one centre-right, the other centre-left. This alliance, called The Democratic Alliance, covered an electoral spectrum sufficiently wide to hope to win against the extreme parties.

Marquet's tactics were simple. He only needed a few points to get through the first round. Allying with parties that were relatively close politically would get him those points. The parties he was allying with, given the latest polls, had no chance of featuring in the second round. By standing with the President, they would join a coalition allowing them to end up on the winning side. Marquet made the necessary concessions both on the Alliance's manifesto and on the composition of the government, ensuring, however, that the negotiations were always carried out with an eye to France's strategic interests. He was determined that the platform the voters were offered should be resolutely innovative, in a range of areas, to capture the electorate's attention.

In truth, he had been considering, in the face of the danger the rise of the extreme parties posed in his view, a much more ambitious project, that of a government of national unity, which would even include the right-wing Republican party, and which would carry still more weight with the electorate. An alliance like that would have been truly exceptional in French politics. He had eventually given up on the idea, so as not to create a gap between the Alliance and the extreme parties, and also because the leader of the Republican Party would not withdraw his candidacy for the presidential election. However, he kept hold of the idea of an electoral agreement for the legislative elections, once the presidential elections were over.

The Alliance's manifesto, the result of intense discussions, included, in addition to further economic and social reforms, a proposal for a fundamental overhaul of the European Union. The President wanted to regain control of Europe's development, and not leave the field to his opponents. But it was above all the disastrous European heads of state and government summit in mid-February, which he attended, that drove him to act decisively, convinced that the Union was heading for catastrophe without far reaching changes. He returned home from this summit absolutely furious. The meeting was supposed to focus on three major topics: the common defence policy, the preparation of a new phase of negotiations at the World Trade Organisation, and a project for the formation of a European Internet giant. The discussions became bogged down, each state defending its own interest tooth and nail. The time set aside for the first two subjects overran substantially without reaching any concrete agreement, and it was not even possible to discuss the great technology project, since several leaders wanted to pre-empt a decision on the location of the Internet giant's headquarters, arguing that their country was obviously best placed to host it. The French president, exasperated with this paralysis, had fortunately managed to hold fruitful discussions on the sidelines with the German Chancellor, a woman of about forty, very pragmatic, favourable to any arrangement which would lead to progress. Together, they agreed that the Union could no longer get twenty-seven countries to move forward uniformly. Marquet brought out an idea he had formulated at the beginning of his term: a Europe with concentric circles, with a tapering integration of countries according to their distance from the central circle. But how could you define these circles without giving rise to endless negotiations? The President quickly realised that even the Chancellor did not share his vision of which countries would form the first core section. Another plan was required. The German leader suggested that he should develop a proposal and discuss it with her and fellow leaders with whom they had a good relationship, over the following weeks. The President had conversations with other heads of government who supported the idea. It was on his return to France, during his negotiations on the Alliance, that he found a formula that he thought would do, based on a European vision that was globally decentralised but allowed for in-depth collaboration. The Alliance's final manifesto provided for a major transformation of Europe, on a basis that would encourage a revival of the Union, which the President and his allies were strongly attached to, while presenting a solid response to the many criticisms raised by the opposition parties.

The Democratic Alliance's overall strategy paid off. It shot ahead in the polls.

★ ★ ★

The French electoral campaign was being watched in Great Britain. Tracy was very interested in the creation of the Democratic Alliance. On the one hand, the proposed reform of Europe warranted close inspection. On the other hand, the method chosen by President Marquet (whose hostile attitude during the Brexit negotiations in 2017-2018 had not been forgotten by Tracy) was interesting: he had turned around a situation where he was cornered, with the prospect of a humiliating electoral defeat, and bounced back with an innovative idea. She now felt herself equally cornered, with her country sinking into a financial crisis with no end in sight.

Tracy had the Democratic Alliance's proposals for the reform of the European Union analysed by her researchers. When she received back the analysis of the proposals she had the strongest feeling they could almost have been written by John Klin! Perhaps because of President Marquet's exasperation, the principle of a Europe composed of sovereign nations was at the heart of the Alliance's proposal. The European institutions were confirmed in a purely drafting role, with States choosing the rules they wanted to apply, with multilateral agreements being encouraged, thus preventing stalemate situations. The European Parliament was to be dissolved. The Council would take a role solely covering coordination between governments. European democratic and social values were reaffirmed as the cement between nations. The four freedoms of movement – of people, goods, capital and services – were confirmed but reframed. Finally, a European defence force would be created. These principles would be validated by a new treaty whose approval would be submitted to the French Parliament. Of course, none of this could be implemented without the agreement of other countries. The project of reforming the European Treaty was thus planned to take place in 2023 with the aim of approval and implementation in 2024.

Tracy thought that a reform like that, had it been implemented in 2016, would perhaps have changed the result of the British vote at the time. Apart from the free movement of persons, which would have to have been subject to negotiation, and European defence, technically difficult to put in place, the rest of the provisions would probably have been acceptable to the British public. Today, even more than in 2016, this reform could pave the way for new negotiations between the United Kingdom and the European Union, and even, who knows, rejoining...

The Prime Minister knew that European countries accepting this reform was far from a done deal, and that there would probably be significant amendments. After weeks of reflection, however, there was no doubt in her mind that the United Kingdom had to rejoin either the European Economic Area or a reformed Union. The experience of Brexit XXL had shown that the British economy, closely linked to that of the Continent, had suffered more than it had benefited from the break-up. In rejecting what she had believed from 2016 to 2021, Tracy was honest enough to recognise the objective results of her policy. True to herself, she analysed her own performance without complacency, but was careful not to reveal her thoughts to anyone.

★ ★ ★

On Friday night, February 25th, for the first time since the beginning of the financial crisis, Tracy decided to take a walk. The route she'd chosen quite randomly for the security services was to go down Whitehall towards Westminster, then take Abingdon Street and back down to the Embankment at Victoria Tower Gardens to walk along the Thames. The return leg would be along the back streets, ending up at Storey's gate and Horse Guards Avenue to Downing Street. The weather was nice but cold. Tracy wrapped up well and left at around 5.30pm. As she was leaving Parliament Street to cross Parliament Square, in front of Westminster, a woman recognised her and came running up to her screaming. Several police officers immediately surrounded Tracy but she signalled to them to let her listen to the woman. She was shouting that the government had ruined her and her husband, by their stupid policies, making them lose all their savings. She was on the verge of hysteria. Tracy wanted to ask her name, to see if her staff could do anything, but the woman just shouted even louder, that the government was doing nothing anyway, that they were all liars. A crowd began to gather, people were filming the scene on their phones, and the bodyguards asked the Prime Minister not to stay. Two policewomen took the woman away in a police van to calm her down. Tracy issued instructions to have the couple's name sent to social services to supervise their case. She wanted to carry on walking but the police dissuaded her and she reluctantly returned to Downing Street. The scene had shocked her, cruelly reminding her of the contrast between her immense responsibility as Prime Minister and her range of action, which was so limited considering the stakes. But she knew no one would understand that.

Demonstrations

Jeremy Jones, known as JJ to his friends, had been Labour Party leader since 2020, so for about two years. He had only started out in politics three years earlier, at the time of the Brexit negotiations in 2017. He had been unemployed at the time, having lost his job because the small carpentry company that employed him went bankrupt. Fortunately his wife was working, which made it possible for the couple and their two young boys to live reasonably well. He was forty-three at the time, tall, blond, naturally bursting with energy, throwing himself into his project with the strength of a former rugby player, and he was quickly taken up by the party. He was given a constituency to stand for in the 2018 general election. He spent several months visiting every market, every shop, almost every house, and especially every pub. He was elected, gaining one of the best results for Labour, which made him famous among his colleagues, many of whom had lost their seats in the midst of the Conservative party's landslide victory.

His passion for politics, discovered late in life, was real. With his strong physique and a booming voice, he delivered impromptu and impassioned speeches, which often left him sweating. People liked his commitment and his easy manner. He was not the most subtle of politicians, but he was a rock, someone who inspired confidence; you always knew where you were with him. He did not like intellectual politicians or the Westminster elite, and did not hide the fact. His credo was the defence of the workers, the employees, the lower middle class, whom he called the true wealth of the country. A convinced European, he said that Britain had nothing to fear from Continental competition; quite the opposite. For him the problem was London, not Brussels. He favoured the European Social Charter and workers' rights. He said Brexit would lead to social dumping, putting employees more at the mercy of bosses. Disconcerted by the feuds amongst party leaders which tore the Labour party apart, leading to its defeat in 2018, he told himself that he couldn't do worse than the rest of them, and began an ascent of the party with his usual passion, as soon as he was elected to the House of Commons. Thanks to his infectious warmth, his enthusiasm and his conviction, in just two years he had managed to find support in almost all sections of the party and was elected leader quite naturally at the beginning of 2020. Since then, he had had a single goal: to get a general election called, beat the Conservatives, put in place an economic policy with a strong social component, and bring the country back into the European Union, or at least within the European Economic Area on the same basis as Norway. He firmly positioned his party as favourable to Europe, putting an end to Labour's traditional ambivalence on this subject.

His favourite target was, of course, Tracy Meller, whom he attacked every Wednesday in Parliament at Prime Minister's Question Time. After the February 2022 crisis, however, he saw that Meller was not going to change her policy, and decided that he needed to do more.

Convinced that the country was heading for ruin under the Conservatives, he believed that there was no time to lose. As the Prime Minister wouldn't call an early General Election, he would have to get people onto the streets. He held discussions with party officials, union leaders, and especially younger party members, who were the most motivated. Relentlessly cataloguing the catastrophic effects of Conservative policies, he convinced many people of the need to take action. Only the trades unions were unconvinced, because they did not want to compromise their work by focussing on political choices, such as the return to Europe, instead of concentrating on purely social and economic issues. Within the party, the support was massive, first because the majority of members were pro-Europe, especially young people, but mostly because everyone felt that the European issue would bring down the Conservatives, making way for Labour to return to power in the next election. February 17th was a trial run. Open to party members and members of sympathetic unions, an event in Hyde Park brought together fifty thousand people. Jones made a speech that fired up the demonstrators, calling again on the government to resign, and appealing to all British people who felt concerned to join the movement in the coming weeks.

The next event was scheduled for Saturday, March 5th. The groundwork was laid with an intensive online campaign. Jeremy Jones did not have much money, and he did not commission much TV or radio advertising. On the other hand, he encouraged young members to use their social networks. The themes were the same: the government should step down, call a General Election, put an end to Conservative policy, implement social justice measures, and return to Europe. They settled on a slogan: "Tories Out, Britain In" (convinced as they were of the necessity above all for these two goals – get rid of the Tories and get back into Europe), sometimes replaced by the more frank "Meller Out, Britain In".

Over the fortnight leading up to the demonstration, the internet was flooded with criticism of government policy and examples of the disastrous effects of the crisis. They published interviews with employees who had been made redundant, retirees who had lost their pensions in the stock market crash, and students deprived of the opportunity to go abroad because the cost had become prohibitive, Construct customers who had lost their deposits, etc... At the same time, articles appeared showing that another way was possible. The press campaign cleverly captured the public's discontent and fear.

A fine rain on Saturday, March 5th did not stop the demonstrators. From eight o'clock in the morning hundreds of people started to pour out of the tube exits around Hyde Park. At noon attendance was estimated at three hundred thousand people, which was Jones' stated goal. The radio and television coverage of the event caught the attention of Londoners, many of whom decided to come. At three o'clock, there were five hundred thousand demonstrators and the police began to worry about crowd safety. Representatives of the party, particularly young people, and from several associations, had been speaking since the morning. The atmosphere was like a festival; snack and hotdog sellers had been lured to the event and were doing a roaring trade. At three thirty, Jeremy Jones spoke, from the stage erected in the middle of the park. His stentorian voice rang out, relayed by an array of loudspeakers.

"This government is driving the country to ruin! In five years, the unemployment rate has doubled and shows no sign of slowing down. Businesses are dropping like flies. Our purchasing power has collapsed, wages have fallen. And what is Mrs Meller doing? She's pledging to carry on with the same policy, the only workable one – according to her!"

The crowd start shouting: "Meller Out!"

"This government wants us to believe that it's good for our products to be taxed entering Europe, good that our young people can't study abroad any more, that our life is better with the pound halved in value, and it's good that foreigners keep away while we hole up here!"

More shouts of "Tories out! Tories out!"

"This government has no social policies. Unemployment benefit has virtually been eliminated, NHS funding has been cut, our schools are getting less public money. This government is not investing in infrastructure! And this government is bankrupt!"

"Tories out! Tories out!"

Jeremy Jones raised his voice still louder.

"We are here to say NO to the government. We are here to say that we want a UK that is open to the world, progressive and social. We want policies that show real solidarity! We don't want any more of the Conservatives' ideological experiments. We have had enough of a Brexit that isolates the country and condemns us to recession. We need a major plan for economic recovery, with large scale investments. We want a Tory exit and re-entry into Europe for Britain!"

The crowd chanted the slogan "Tories Out, Britain In!".

"We demand the government resigns, and we demand elections so that the British people can decide on their destiny!"

The crowd shouted "An election! We demand an election!".

"My friends, this day is the beginning of a great struggle! It marks the beginning of the rebirth of the country. After five years of suffocation under Conservative policies, the British people will be free. After the Tory lies, the nation needs to hear the truth! We're going to continue our demonstrations every week for as long as necessary, until Mrs Meller hears us and until we achieve our goal: a general election, which we will win!"

Jones ended his speech to wild applause from the crowd. His speech was the end of the political component for the day, but a concert was planned to follow. Many people stayed to make the most of the day, especially since the drizzle had stopped. The last participants did not leave until late in the evening.

Jones knew that he had just embarked on a historic battle, the most important of his life, and that the first step had been a success. The demonstrations became a weekly fixture. Organised only in Hyde Park the first couple of times, they began to take place in several cities simultaneously from the following Saturday, including in Wales, Scotland and Northern Ireland. On the last Saturday in March, there were one million protesters across the country. The Conservative Party worried about the size of the movement. Guy Wick, without the government's approval, decided that a counter-attack was necessary.

Guy Wick takes action

In 2018, the Conservative Party had won a brilliant election victory on the platform of Brexit XXL. At the time, Britain's new independent policy had been documented, argued over, broken down into measurable objectives; it had been the subject of innumerable speeches, media interviews and electoral leaflets. The electorate were promised it as the solution that would give the country a bright future, and it had become, in a few months, a kind of dogma. This political direction, fuelled by almost two years of frustrating negotiations with Europe, seemed inevitable to party members. In 2018, there were few in the party who were not favourable to Brexit, and even fewer who did not want the most absolute form, that is, a complete break with Europe.

Members, and especially the executive, knew that the transition would be tricky. They expected some economic ups and downs. But no one would have predicted that after four years, Britain would be facing one of the worst financial crises in its history.

In 2022, despite all the difficulties, only a minority, about a third, regretted their choice. The majority calculated that sooner or later the future would vindicate Brexit XXL. For these members, represented by Guy Wick, Jeremy Jones' protests were very annoying. As the month of March went on, the more the demonstrations increased, the more the irritation grew in the ranks of the party. There was no question of the popular movement trying by force to invalidate a policy that had been doubly determined by democratic means – in the 2016 referendum and the general elections of 2018. It was also very irksome that the government, and in particular, Tracy Meller, remained essentially passive in the face of these demonstrations.

Guy Wick, for many, was the man for the job. A born politician, ready to use any methods to achieve his ends, capable of verbal violence against his opponents, possessing a resolute and courageous character, this fifty-three year-old former lawyer had headed the pro-Brexit XXL wing since 2018. Everyone knew he was just waiting for an opportunity to bring down Tracy Meller. Party officials and members alike were beginning to grow tired of the Prime Minister. Admittedly, Meller had given them one of their biggest electoral victories. She had invented the concept of Brexit XXL, and had had the courage to implement it. But for several months now, they had been forced to admit that the results were not forthcoming. They smelled procrastination and hesitation. Now, a party does not want a hesitant leader, especially if she seems to be questioning one of its fundamental doctrines. Members want an executive leader who engages everyone along clear lines. So the idea was starting to spread that a change of leadership might be a good thing, and that Guy Wick would do just fine.

The pretender chose a strategy that allowed him both to attack Jeremy Jones and dissociate himself from the government. Holding fast to his original plan, he wanted Tracy Meller to fall, but not before the end of the year. This would involve a gradually increasing pressure, avoiding mass demonstrations before September, when the real attack would begin. So Wick began by holding back, while members of his party urged him to launch a gigantic counter-demonstration. In two speeches to the party at the end of March, he openly criticised Jeremy Jones for daring to call on people to take to the streets, when the country was in financial turmoil. "You don't demonstrate when the stock market is collapsing, when people are losing their savings, when companies are going bankrupt every day, and the country is facing one of the worst crises it has ever seen!"

Openly accusing the Labour leader of working against the country's interests, Wick claimed that the Conservative party had a sense of responsibility and was focused on the sole priority of the moment, the recovery of the economy. He launched online petitions demanding the end of the demonstrations. This campaign, efficient, and well publicised in the media, had a definite effect. Jeremy Jones, accused of opportunistically taking advantage of the country's situation to serve his personal ends, was briefly put off balance. He explained of course that the crisis was the work of the Conservative Party and not his doing, but the blow had hit home. Attendance at Labour rallies dropped in April. Wick's position had a secondary advantage, that of issuing constant reminders that the country was in a very serious situation, which was a way of criticising the government without appearing to.

On April 14th, Guy Wick went to France, ostensibly to support the nationalist party ten days before the first round of presidential elections. His dream was obviously that the right wing party should win, because once France left Europe, the European Union would collapse and there would be no risk that any British government, of whatever stripe, could propose renewed membership. When questioned by voters who were still worried about the consequences of leaving the Union, he replied that the situation was temporarily difficult because Great Britain was alone, as a bellwether on the road to independence, but if other countries followed, it would become easier.

However, he had calculated that despite all efforts, the nationalist party would not win the elections. This meant that the Democratic Alliance would come to power, bringing with it a project for the reform of Europe. Wick saw this reform as a deadly threat to Brexit: in Britain's current economic situation, the prospect of a "flexible Union" (as it was referred to by the press once the Alliance's proposal became known), in which nations would retain their sovereignty, might become very attractive and particularly difficult to combat. But the Conservative grandee had only one credo: total independence for Britain, no membership of any kind of union, even a flexible one. Only the Commonwealth found favour with him. His analysis was that the proposed reformed European political structure was a sham: sooner or later the bureaucracy would regain control and we would return to the same old problems, or even a yet more complex situation resulting from relaxation of the common regulations. So there was no question of Britain joining a project like that. The reform presented no risk in the short term, as its implementation, even supposing that it was supported by other governments, could technically not be realised before 2024, at the earliest, given the ratification timetable necessary for a change of treaty from each member country of the Union. But, in the near future, Jeremy Jones, and perhaps Tracy Meller, would seize the idea, place it at the heart of the national political debate and present it as the ideal solution to the British dilemma: access to the European market without the constraints. Wick decided that he had to combat this concept. When party members again suggested organising mass demonstrations, he replied that the people were not ready and that they were going to have to use different tactics to prepare the ground.

In mid-April, with the support of some sections of the media, he embarked on phase 2 of his plan, which consisted of a smear campaign on Europe. A puppet show, similar to the much-missed *Spitting Image*, was created: four times a week, European leaders were portrayed tearing each other apart, one day over the budget, the next day on the Common Agricultural Policy, the third day on immigration, the fourth day on the harmonisation of employment law, the fifth day on the measures to be taken to save the Euro, and so on. The show, which was well made and funny, was broadcast on social networks, to a sizeable audience and conveyed a simple message: Europe was a nest of vipers we'd do well to steer clear of. This show, despite its cartoonish nature, contributed to further destabilisation for Jeremy Jones. When he mentioned Europe in his speeches, his audience couldn't help envisaging the show's puppets, and hilarity ensued, even amongst his most convinced supporters.

Wick felt satisfied with the first few weeks of his plan. He had managed to scale back the Labour protests, embarrass Jeremy Jones, point out the Prime Minister's inefficiency, and sow doubts in the public's mind about the desirability of a return to Europe, all without having wheeled out his big guns – which he planned for September.

Jeremy Jones, however, was not one for giving up. In May he decided to change tactics. They were going to have to take a break from the big demonstrations, on the one hand because the decline in attendance was starting to show, on the other hand because they were an ongoing logistical nightmare. Using the party's youth members, he launched Red Spots. Instead of meeting in one central place in every city, the protesters now had the choice of dozens or even hundreds of public places: at a given time, they would turn up at one of the "Red Spots", and take a selfie or a video, or just check in. These Red Spots were public squares or parks, but also often pubs, restaurants or libraries, whose managers had agreed to participate in the campaign. A downloadable mobile app identified Red Spots near your location, as well as timetabled slots, such as "The Red

Lion Pub, between 12pm and 5pm". Once there, the protesters registered their participation with a single click, and could then upload their photos or videos. The application indicated in real time the number of people at each Red Spot as well as the total number of daily participants. This system was extremely flexible, there were plenty of Red Spots, and the time slots were fairly long, which was nice and convenient. The vast majority of the country's pubs and restaurants agreed to become Red Spots, given the level of customers it attracted for them, and offered cheap set menus to appeal to most of their visitors. So instead of gathering a million people in a few places at the same time, which was complex, Jeremy Jones was swiftly able to gather the same number of people in tens of thousands of Red Spots throughout the country, and with virtually no logistical issues. The method was a storming success: people appreciated the flexibility of the system but also its user-friendly nature – conversations sprang up naturally between groups who found themselves in the same places, something which was much harder at the mass events. The Red Spots became places for debate and many restaurants were saved from bankruptcy in May and June by this unexpected boost. Guy Wick couldn't find a way of complaining about the new method of demonstrating: the participants didn't seem to be obstructing the streets or creating disorder while the country was suffering, as they were contributing to the revenues of the locations they visited. On the other hand the mini-debates taking place allowed the discussion to rise above the caricatured image of the movement and Europe that the puppet show had fostered. From mid-June, the puppets stopped being viral and their appeal began to wane.

* * *

For several weeks there had been one very disgruntled spectator of the Wick-Jones match. Namely, Tracy. She was fiercely critical of the Labour leader in Parliament in March, accusing him of using undemocratic methods – mob rule – to achieve political goals.

"Wait until the elections in 2023," she said, "and you can campaign within legitimate electoral rules!"

However, deep down she understood perfectly well the game Jones was playing: he was in opposition, he had to criticise the government, he needed to make as much noise as possible; it was annoying but par for the course. What she had a lot more trouble accepting was Wick's attitude. She knew how ambitious he was and knew very well that he was laying the groundwork for an attempt to unseat her. But more than that, she was disgusted by his methods: instead of engaging in a frank and direct debate with Jones, he was using devious means – smears and media manipulation. She did not believe these kinds of methods served the Brexit cause. The government's policy did not need underhand defence; it could very well be openly explained and discussed. The Prime Minister discussed this problem with several party officials, but they were hesitant to act against Wick, because they could see the effectiveness of the methods used, even if they did not like them. Many of them were afraid of Wick and did not want to be the target of his venomous verbal attacks.

Tracy thought her best strategy would be to bide her time. She could confront Jones in debate, at the right moment, i.e. during the run-up to the next elections. As for Wick, she knew from experience that one day he would go too far and annoy too many people. That day would herald his fall. For now, the main thing was to focus on government action. The financial crisis had to be resolved, without allowing herself to be distracted by other events. In May, the Democratic Alliance won the French presidential elections and looked set to win the legislative elections. Lessons would have to be learnt from this. As Brexit had affected France, France was going to affect Great Britain with its new political landscape. It was the same for Germany, the other great European nation, which had finally elected a strong majority government in 2021.

On June 7th, however, the Prime Minister received very bad news. Laura Soriens telephoned her around 4pm to tell her that HGB was about to go bankrupt. The bank had not been able to stand up to the repeated blows that had been hammering it for months: the financial crisis of January, the collapse of Construct, the stock market crash of February, Merlin bank going into administration, the increasing level of defaults on payment from creditors who had sunk into financial trouble. Tracy felt a strong sense of personal guilt listening to the CEO's explanations: the economies of other European countries were not booming, but they were all in a state of relative growth and their financial markets were functional. Was she right to carry on her chosen path? Instead of the brief storm she had planned for, had she steered the country into the heart of a much more violent hurricane, as Jeremy Jones said? Had she mismanaged the situation? She knew that Laura Soriens was an experienced manager. If her bank had not managed to carry on, it could have been due to some past mistakes, but there was more to it. Something in the system was broken. Could the country cope with this new ordeal?

The Chief Executive told her that the Bank of England had been warned, and that Philip Denniel himself was looking into possible solutions with the help of the Chancellor of the Exchequer. "All these people have known for several hours and no one has thought to warn me," ruminated the Prime Minister. "Why am I the last to know?" She invited the Chief Executive to meet her as a matter of urgency at Downing Street with her Chairman, where they would organise a meeting with the

Chancellor. They would have to act quickly. When she had put the phone down, she couldn't shake the impression that implicit throughout the call had been a question from Laura Soriens – "Why didn't you change direction after February? Why are you letting the country carry on in this state?" She knew the political answer to this question, but couldn't rid herself of her anxiety.

In any event, the HGB bankruptcy would be a disaster that they needed to try to avoid at all costs.

Tired but determined, she telephoned the Chancellor.

Janet Gradens

Janet Gradens was the woman who had shouted abuse at the Prime Minister in Parliament Square. She had been arrested by the police and taken to one of their vehicles parked nearby, where a police woman had spoken to her at length, managing to calm her down. Janet had cried and explained that she'd been affected by the financial difficulties she was in. After a caution, and her promise not to do it again, she had been released.

Her story was tragic. Janet suffered from mental illness, and was prone to fits and paranoia. She had been sectioned several times around 2006-2008, when she was in her early twenties. With good care, she had been discharged, if not cured, at least sufficiently balanced to be able, according to the doctors, to live normally. She had no parents or extended family or friends to support her. She found jobs in shops, often taken advantage of by bosses who paid her very little. She was quite pretty with a slender figure and beautiful black hair she wore long. Her soft-featured face had penetrating eyes, which were always lit with energy. When she was well, she was good natured and customers appreciated her. Her first months of work with a new employer were generally good. Unfortunately, after a while, there would always be an incident which sent her into a rage. Once, when she was working in a shoe shop, her manager had accused her of carelessness in stocktaking and reordering shoes. The discussion had escalated, Janet got carried away, accused the manager of hiding the shoes so as to be able to blame her later, and suddenly she was chucking shoes at his head. He finally overpowered her, but then fired her. When this kind of incident occurred, Janet was plunged into depression for several weeks, then moved house to another area, found another job, and made a fresh start.

She thought she had found happiness when in 2015 she met Patrick Gills. Patrick was a delivery driver at the greengrocer where she worked. At twenty-six, he was two years younger than her. He was attracted to her, and unaware of her mental instability, pursued her keenly. Janet, who up till then had only had disappointing romantic encounters, was quickly conquered by this handsome young redhead, strong and always smiling. The couple got married a few months later. The young woman, carried along by her new-found happiness, went through one of the calmest periods of her life, not experiencing any manic episodes. After two months, Patrick, tired of being an employee at the whim of his bosses, decided to open a small pizzeria having inherited some money when his mother had died suddenly. Janet gave him all her meagre savings and they embarked on the adventure. The pizzeria, located in Canary Wharf, London's modern business district, was an immediate success. It didn't make them a fortune, but allowed them to live decently, putting some money aside.

From the end of 2016, however, there was a slowdown in business activity in the financial institutions of Canary Wharf, a direct result of the Brexit vote. A lot of the employees of these companies used to have their lunch at the pizzeria. They would talk at the table about the offshore outsourcing that their companies planned and complain about government policy. Little by little, the number of customers dwindled. Where Janet and Patrick served sixty covers at lunch each day in early 2016, the number had halved by late 2017 and fell to twenty in 2018-2019. The couple gradually let the employees go, eventually doing all the work themselves. That allowed them to hold on through 2020-2021 despite the still dropping level of business. The situation became very difficult in January 2022. Janet and Patrick could no longer cover the rent of the pizzeria. They had reduced all possible costs but could not cope any more. The February financial crisis was the death blow. The banks were making large scale redundancies. Patrick became nervous; life with Janet was increasingly difficult. She was prone once again to fits of temper, first occasionally and then frequently.

In an insidious way, an obsession took root in Janet's head: the Prime Minister was responsible for their difficulties. She had often heard it said by the bankers having lunch at the pizzeria. On February 23rd, under terrible stress from their inability to meet the rent for the second month running, she decided to act. She decided to see the Prime Minister to pour out her grievances about her policies. Without saying anything to Patrick, she took the Tube to near Downing Street. Tracy Meller's walking habits were well known and Janet planned to take advantage of one of these outings to talk to her. But on the 23rd, Tracy did not go out. On the 24th, Janet returned, pacing up and down Whitehall and Parliament Square again, still without success. On the 25th, she was late. She came out of Westminster tube station quickly and as she crossed Parliament Street, she was surprised to see that the Prime Minister, whom she recognised from the television, was preparing to walk into Parliament Square a few yards away. Janet didn't hesitate but immediately approached her, shouting. She was surprised at the Prime Minister's attitude and willingness to listen to her without sheltering behind the police. However, she was too upset to contain herself. She only succeeded in shouting that the government was useless, that they were leading the country into disaster, that they had ruined her and her husband. She became almost hysterical. When the police took her away, she starting screaming in earnest and thought she was going to be put in prison. Her arrest must have been the Prime Minister's doing, and she yelled accusations of treason at her. It was only in the police car that she calmed down, taken in hand by an experienced policewoman. She was released a few hours later, and returned home at dawn. To explain her absence, she told Patrick that one of her friends had been in an accident, and that she had had to accompany her to the hospital. Patrick did not ask questions. For the last few weeks, it had been him who frequently went out at night, often for no good reason. When Janet asked where he had gone, he would get angry, saying he needed free time to de-stress. The evening would end in an argument.

After three more very difficult months, Patrick closed the pizzeria at the end of May, and declared it insolvent. The couple spent a few days emptying the premises and reselling as much of the equipment as they could, using the money to repay the most pressing debts. Janet fell into a depression, spending hours at the pizzeria in a dazed state, working slowly. Patrick took charge of the work, delivering the equipment they had sold in a small van. He did not return at night all week, claiming the journeys took up all his time. Janet spent her evenings in front of the television, eating junk. It was Friday, at the end of the week, the last Friday of May, that her world finally collapsed. As they had at last finished clearing out the pizzeria, she went to do some shopping for the evening meal. When she returned to the flat, she did not see Patrick, which was normal. But his things were gone too. On the table was a short note on ruled paper: Patrick told her that he was leaving her. Janet screamed, knocked over the table and the chairs, rushed out into the street, calling her husband – but the van was gone. She tried to reach him on his mobile phone, but there was no answer. She returned to the flat and collapsed on the bed, screaming and crying.

Several hours later, having calmed down somewhat after her fit of nerves, she turned on the television, mechanically. It was the evening news. And there was Tracy Meller, explaining that Britain was going through a difficult economic phase, but that the government had taken action and that the country would come through it.

"Die, you bitch!" Janet shouted, throwing her shoes at the television. "You've destroyed everything! You should just die!" Over the weeks that followed, the young woman fell into a state of nervous exhaustion. She hardly went out of the house, spending her days in bed. A nagging idea grew in the back of her mind: if she took action, very public action, to rid the country of the one person most responsible for landing it in such trouble, Patrick would come back to her. This idea, devoid of any rational logic, became an obsession: she had to kill Tracy Meller. She could have done it the other day if she had had a knife and if she had thought to, if she had acted quickly. It's not illegal to walk around with a knife in your pocket. Besides, who would notice? Wrapped up in her sheets, Janet began to construct scenarios.

Campaign Strategies

On Saturday June 25th, 2022, Jeremy Jones organised the last Red Spot before the summer break. He had decided to put the protest movement on hold for July and August to avoid campaign fatigue setting in, and planned to restart with a major event on 17th September.

Nearly five months after the beginning of the financial crisis, the country was in a very risky situation. There was an increasing number of bankruptcies, affecting small businesses, like the Canary Wharf pizzeria, as well as large commercial, industrial or financial enterprises. The government, at Tracy's instigation, supported by the Governor of the Bank of England, had provided an urgent recapitalisation of HGB Bank, saving it from insolvency by nationalising it, but could not do the same for all the smaller companies. There was widespread anxiety. Apart from Jeremy Jones' Red Spots, there were a series of demonstrations organised by unions or support networks for the unemployed or those in crisis. There had been a rash of incidents where the police had had to intervene. The political gap was widening between Labour supporters and those of Guy Wick's movement. Those backing Tracy Meller, however, could be counted on the fingers of one hand.

Guy Wick was not planning to take a break during the summer. He knew he had fewer followers than Jeremy Jones. They were also more difficult to mobilise, given the apparent failure of Brexit. This was the reason (apart, of course, from his own personal ambitions) why, against the advice of many in his party, he had not launched large scale demonstrations sooner. He had calculated that a gradual escalation would be required. He was aware that grassroots support for Brexit continued to be strong, as several unpublished polls, which he had commissioned, had confirmed for him. To rouse this support base, he would need to start making speeches, and, although he had made several during the first part of the year, he felt it was necessary to move up a gear now, after the months of preparatory work in April and May. In mid-June, he decided to start the third phase of his action plan. Visiting two or three groups every week, he would cover several towns across the country over the course of the summer, particularly those who had voted in the largest numbers for Brexit. He would make rousing speeches to motivate his supporters. The campaign would build up to a huge demonstration in September, which his supporters were eagerly awaiting.

* * *

Nick Walderg lost his job at HGB Bank in mid-June, as part of the massive restructuring carried out by Laura Soriens under the emergency rescue plan agreed with the government. Still in shock, Nick decided to participate in the Red Spot event on June 25th. It was easy for him as he only had to go to The Unicorn, a pub fifteen minutes' walk from home. Then he was going to meet Nancy late in the afternoon to see a film. He left his flat on Stanley Crescent at about two o'clock, went down Stanley Gardens, turned right into Kensington Park Road, then into the first street on the left. A few minutes later he reached Pembridge Square Garden, one of his favourite spots. It was a lovely warm day and a pleasure to walk through London under the clear blue skies. Nick saw children having fun in the square, people walking their dogs, a squirrel climbing a tree. Continuing on down Moscow Road, he reached Queensway, where the pub was located. The place was already crowded, and discussions were well underway on the economic and political situation as well as on other subjects.

Nick ordered a pint at the bar. While registering on the Red Spots app, he looked around. The customers were mainly young, dressed for the warm weather. Nick noticed a group of four people, probably in their thirties, two women and two men – two couples perhaps – who were chatting and enjoying ice creams. They were in gales of laughter as one of them did a ridiculous impression of Guy Wick fulminating about The European Menace. It was clear from their conversation that the four customers were die hard Remainers. Behind their laughter, Nick sensed frustration, unless on the other hand what he was perceiving was their sense that the last days of Brexit were nigh, and that soon they could start laughing about the nightmare. Nick overheard other conversations, employees who had just lost their jobs or who were struggling. Many were glad of the Red Spot campaign – it gave them an outlet for their feelings. They read out the comments they had posted on the app: "Keep on going JJ!", "Save this country", "Brexit XXL, XXL problems!" "Meller is bleeding us dry!" and so on... A lot of people were talking about other topics, though: the latest sports events, their next holiday, the summer styles. Nick noticed three people eating at another table. They were three men whom he guessed were in their forties. Their conversation was quite different: they were saying that it was essential to forge on with Brexit at all costs, even if the current situation was dire, because the benefits of economic freedom would be reaped after the financial adjustment. They were quite well dressed, and Nick thought maybe they were executives at one of the companies taking advantage of the situation. There was a couple behind them, a little older, enjoying fish and chips at a small table next to the window. Nick couldn't hear what this couple was saying, but they did not seem to be sharing the general mood. The young man was distracted by three pretty girls in short skirts and t-shirts who had just come into the pub and were ordering soft drinks at the bar. Nick watched them check in on their mobiles. They took a laughing selfie for the app, talked for a bit about Jeremy Jones, whose energy they liked, and then changed the subject to discuss their plans for the first day of Wimbledon the following Monday. Once again Nick was struck by the contrast between the disastrous general economic situation and the almost carefree atmosphere in public places. Four young guys in their twenties came in, making quite a racket. They ordered beers and started chatting up the girls, but the girls managed to ditch them quite neatly, after a bit of banter, by going to sit at a small table. The four young men left them alone and began to wander around the pub, beers in hand. They were approaching drinkers and, under cover of sharing the messages they had sent on the app, asking to see what people had written. Most people were happy to oblige. The three executives openly expressed their pro-Brexit views. An argument started, with the young men becoming aggressive. The toughest one raised his voice; he was telling the executives to "clear off". He said that the country was not going to carry on following people who were leading it into disaster, and shouted that Leavers were not welcome in this pub today. People started telling them to calm down and have some respect for the other customers, but to no avail. The executives got up to face off the young men spoiling for a fight. They angrily declared that the pub was a public place and that they had no intention of leaving. One of the girls Nick had spotted let out a scream as the four young men suddenly jumped on the executives and started trying to violently throw them out. Nick tried to intervene but got a punch in the face for his troubles, which broke his nose. With his face covered in blood, he went back to the bar where a barman passed him a towel. He saw the four strong young men forcing the executives out of the pub, then running straight off, as the landlord called the police. The fuss had only lasted a few minutes, but the pub was in chaos. The older man eating with his wife stood up, outraged, and shouted to the rest of the customers, "If that's how you want to treat us, don't think we're going to put up with it! We'll fight back and defend our country against this!" Some people tried to calm him down, but nothing helped; the couple left, indignant. All the customers vacated the pub in the next few minutes after paying for their drinks. Nick did the same and went to the nearest walk-in clinic after calling Nancy.

In the evening, on the news, they heard that about thirty similar incidents had occurred in a number of Red Spots during the afternoon. There were no serious injuries. In one case a knife fight was narrowly avoided, which could have been much more serious. The scenario was identical in all cases. Participants in the Red Spot campaign had challenged Leavers at the check-in location, and a fight had ensued. Jeremy Jones' Red Spot initiative lost a lot of credibility because of the violence. On News at 10, the Labour leader apologised, but said he didn't understand, that it was the work of rogue elements who were completely out of tune with the spirit of the movement. He announced the suspension of the Red Spots for the summer, while he planned new ways to demonstrate, to be launched in September.

People who had been attacked also went on TV. They all had the same message: this was no time to leave the field open to opponents of Brexit, who wanted to impose their views by undemocratic means. Brexit supporters needed to mobilise and show that they were not prepared to accept a change in the country's strategic direction. The older man from Nick's pub also appeared, declaring bluntly that he would join a protest as soon as the Conservative Party gave the signal.

One man watched the evening news with great satisfaction. Sitting comfortably in his flat on Caroline Terrace, Guy Wick had kept out of the media spotlight this Saturday. The time for his speeches would come over the next few days. The pro-Brexit movement was beginning to react. Guy Wick poured himself a dram of good whisky to celebrate the day's results.

A turbulent summer

On Monday, June 27th, in the middle of the afternoon, Janet Gradens took the Tube from Canary Wharf dressed in running gear. Thirty minutes and one tube change later, she got off at Embankment Station. She had not chosen Westminster tube although it was closer to Downing Street; she had bad memories of what had happened there on February 25th. When she got to the top of the escalators and saw two police officers, she began to shake, clutching the long-bladed knife she had brought with her through her pocket. If they questioned her, she was going to explain that she had just bought it for her kitchen; she had deliberately left the supermarket label on it. Heart thumping, she passed the two policemen, who did not look at her, and continued on her way to the exit. Her plan was simple: to station herself in St James's Park. She was sure that, sooner or later, Tracy Meller would go for a walk there because she had resumed her old habits, and the park was one of the closest to Downing Street. No one would question Janet if she was going for a walk, like many of the office workers around there, but pacing up and down outside Downing Street would inevitably attract the attention of the security services. She planned to come as often as necessary until she could make her move. Once Tracy Meller was in sight, whether it was today, tomorrow, or another day, she would arrange to pass her going in the opposite direction, pretending to jog, and all of a sudden, she would stab her in the stomach then in the neck. It would only take a few seconds, which would be enough because the Prime Minister's bodyguards were always two or three yards behind. She had no clear idea of what would happen next: she supposed the bodyguards would force her to the ground with her hands behind her back. She hoped to have time to see the face of her dying victim and shout to her that she was doing this to save the country. She had read a book about knife attacks on famous people. Clement the monk killing Henry III of France, Ravaillac assassinating Henry IV, Charlotte Corday stabbing Marat in his bathtub: these had become her heroes. Like them, she would be famous. Her photo would be in all the newspapers the next day. She would go to prison but Patrick, admiring her actions, would come to visit her and wait for her to be released, and they would be together. Her biggest fear was ending up like Damiens, who had wasted his opportunity by only wounding Louis XV. Strangely, no English sovereign or Prime Minister had ever perished by a single assassin's knife in modern history as far as she knew. One more reason for her to go down in history...

★ ★ ★

Meanwhile, in her office at 10 Downing Street, Tracy was working with the Foreign Secretary. They were preparing for the G20 summit which was to be held the following Monday and Tuesday in Berlin. The Prime Minister planned to use this meeting to move forward on the interim arrangements. Their renewal was being held up in Brussels, and it was urgent to resolve the issues before the end of September. Another important matter she wanted to address was to discuss with the French President details of the reform he was proposing for

Europe and to ascertain the points of view of the other heads of government, particularly that of the German Chancellor. She had timetabled a series of bilateral meetings with her colleagues, on the sidelines of the official G20 programme, which was devoted to macroeconomic topics and climate provisions.

After a four-hour planning meeting, she felt sufficiently prepared. She had reviewed most of the topics and debated the negotiating tactics to use, weighing the pros and cons of each argument with her Foreign Secretary. The first discussions would be held with the German Chancellor, then with the French President. The recent attitudes of these two leaders boded well for constructive debate, even if the subject was somewhat delicate.

As it was known that she wanted to hold talks, the main British political players had already taken positions on the summit. There was no disagreement between the parties on the matter of the temporary arrangements, which everyone understood was important. On the other hand, Guy Wick had already denounced any attempt to discuss the European reform plans, saying that "this subject is of no interest to Great Britain". Jeremy Jones had supported the principle of talks between heads of government but said that Tracy Meller was very badly positioned to lead them. In truth, he did not want to let the Prime Minister occupy the high ground on the question of a return to Europe. The reform proposed by the French president seemed to him an ideal solution, which he intended to put at the heart of his manifesto in the next elections.

At about six o'clock Tracy said goodbye to her Minister, and, wanting to make the most of the good weather, prepared to go out for a walk. She called her Head of Security to confirm that day's route, through St James's Park and continuing on to Hyde Park. She needed a long walk for some peace to think over all the topics she would have to discuss the following week.

Since the incident in February she had taken some precautions so as to be less easily recognised. As the weather was fine, she put on sunglasses, a hat, and wore light clothes. She could have been any tourist enjoying a beautiful day in London.

When she entered the park, followed by her two bodyguards in plain clothes, Janet Gradens, sitting on a bench a hundred yards away, spotted her immediately. The young woman thought to herself that fate was smiling on her. She watched Tracy for a moment, then began to walk briskly northwards into the park on a parallel path. Her goal was to overtake her, then go back towards her, appearing to be a keen jogger. The park was busy at this time, with Londoners lured outside by the pleasant temperature at the end of the working day. There were families with children and dogs, couples and lots of runners. Janet decided that was also a good sign: she would move unnoticed amongst the people walking in the park.

* * *

Tracy was aware of the risk she was taking by going on her walks. The security services had argued with her at length when they tried to dissuade her at the beginning of her term of office. Risk of verbal and physical attack, risk of kidnapping, terrorist risk: everything had had to be gone over. The security team had declared that they could not secure this kind of outing in public spaces. But she had not changed her ways. Risk was part of life: she could just as easily have a car accident, a plane crash, suffer a heart attack or have a serious illness. In a way, she was fatalistic: if these things were going to happen, well, then, they would happen. She did not want to live in a permanent security bubble. If a Prime Minister can't walk freely in the heart of the country's capital, then that is the sign of a bigger problem. She trusted in British society and wanted to demonstrate her trust. Her life was dedicated to the country. Besides, hadn't she been right? Nothing serious had happened in five years. On the contrary, she'd had many useful encounters with ordinary citizens. Several had given her food for thought, to the point of leading her to change some of her policies. She had never been afraid. The most alarming incident had been when a near-hysterical woman had approached her, shouting, and the police had intervened very quickly. An inner confidence drove her on. She trusted in fate. It couldn't end now, like that, in the heart of London.

Watching her from afar, Janet Gradens was also thinking about fate. She made a mental note of the distance between the Prime Minister and her bodyguards. A couple of yards, as she had expected. That would be enough. Her time had come.

* * *

Tracy's thoughts at the end of her working day covered not only Monday's summit, but the forthcoming deadlines. The British General Elections were to be held no later than the following May. Was she going to stand? On what platform? A serious change of direction was required in the national policy, and it was particularly important to seize the opportunity of a European reform. The question was whether the country, after the February crisis, was finally ready to hear that approach. Of course, the pro-Europe faction, according to the polls, were now in the majority, and the Labour Party also looked to be taking an unprecedented lead. But Tracy did not want to put an end to Brexit based on a simple majority decision as Jones proposed. That would leave the country divided and not solve the underlying problem. What mattered to her was that the majority of the population needed to be convinced of the choices to be made, even if there would always be some diehards. In February she had felt that political consensus was impossible. She still thought it would be difficult today. But after the economic turbulence of recent months, she considered it was at least possible to prepare the ground with a public opinion that had been severely shaken. There was enough time before the elections to develop a convincing new set of policies. One fundamental difficulty remained insoluble, however: with Guy Wick's movement to the right of her and Jeremy Jones' activists to the left of her, it would be almost impossible for her to gain a majority. The government's poor record and unpopularity, amidst the recession which the country could not shake off, would make any political move that it championed unconvincing.

While Tracy was thinking this, Janet Gradens, at the top of St James's Park, near the Mall, had passed her by. Janet was walking fast, and her heart was thumping. Her anxiety was taking hold. She had to control herself, to get a grip of her nerves; above all she could not give in to one of the panic attacks to which she was prone. She looked down the path and saw Tracy walking along the lakeside, followed as ever by two policemen, and was surprised at that moment that she didn't feel hatred for the woman who had triggered so many of her fits of rage for weeks with her TV appearances. At the moment of taking action, she was thinking only of the task at hand. She remembered her father, in the yard of the farm where she had grown up, who had asked her for help catching an out of control dog which risked attacking the livestock. Together, armed with pitchforks, they had carried out a pincer movement to trap the dog in a corner. Her father had told her where to go and told her to stay calm. Her heart had been beating very fast that day too. When the retreating dog was trapped in the corner of the yard, her father had gone up to it and hit it with his pitchfork. You're allowed to kill to get rid of something dangerous, he had said. Even now, Janet remembered the blood and she started shivering. In a few moments, she would need to start her run up, jog about fifty yards, then turn left, go down to the lake, take the path beside the water back towards Meller to approach her from the front. Then she would strike, without hesitation, as she had seen her father do. Thinking over the route, she calculated that her approach would take less than a minute, according to her reconnaissance that afternoon. She gripped the knife in her pocket and looked around. Her anxiety rocketed. Had the police spotted her? A man and a woman had passed close by her staring at her, about an hour ago. She had lost sight of them at the time, but now they were opposite her again, near the park exit for Buckingham Palace. They were staring at her, she was sure of it. The woman seemed to be coming towards her. Janet, sweating and trembling, began to jog. Don't panic. Don't fall. Follow the path. Her direction was taking her right towards the couple; she had to not look, play the part of a runner focussing on her training. Another twenty yards and she would be very close. Her heart was pounding. Please god let the knife not have fallen out of my pocket. She fumbled around its hiding place and felt the handle. She had to turn, not carry on towards this couple who were exerting a terrible fascination over her. She turned left, began to go down towards the lake. She couldn't see them anymore. In less than a few dozen seconds, she would strike. She would save the country from the danger that threatened it. She reached the lake and took the path to the left. And there was Meller, further along the lake, no more than fifty yards away. It was Meller's fault the pizzeria had gone bust. Meller's fault Patrick had left. Janet ran faster. She wasn't even thinking anymore; all that mattered was reaching the target. She ran faster and faster, another twenty yards till she reached the Prime Minister. What was this man doing with his dog in the middle of the path? Get out of the way, I have to get through! Panting, very angry, Janet almost got tangled in the leash trying to slip between the man and the barking dog. She freed herself, looked up and saw Meller, only three yards away. Two more steps, and she would strike, with all her strength, all her hatred, all her desire to do the dazzling deed that would bring Patrick back to her. She couldn't see the Prime Minister's eyes, hidden behind sunglasses. She had to strike now. Her hand went to her pocket. Suddenly she felt two arms grab strongly round her and stop her in mid-stride. Trapped, unable to move forward, she turned her head and realized that it was the man with the dog, who was holding her tight.

"Sorry, Madam, Police, I'm detaining you for security reasons."

She saw Tracy Meller instantly surrounded by her bodyguards and four other men and taken away. The policeman removed the knife from Janet's pocket.

"What are you doing with this knife?" he asked, still holding her fast.

Janet started shouting.

"Nothing! Nothing! I'm running, this is a kitchen knife that I bought because I broke mine yesterday. Look, the label's still on it!"

"Come with me please," said the man.

Janet saw Tracy Meller walking away. She screamed in the policeman's face: "Let me go, you have no right to arrest people for no reason!"

But there were several police officers around her now. She recognised the man and woman who had stared at her earlier. Shaking, thrashing, she fainted.

★ ★ ★

What had happened was like something out of a James Bond film. The British secret services were not satisfied with two bodyguards and a prior notification of the Prime Minister's itinerary, as they had said. Unbeknownst to Tracy, there were more like twenty police officers who were mobilised every time she went for a walk. Dressed in plain clothes, equipped with the most advanced technology, including miniaturised drones, and armed, they surrounded her, some close up and some further away, and constantly patrolled the surroundings of the route she followed. Sometimes they were the passers-by whom Tracy talked to. Here in St James's Park, every visitor was secretly photographed and identified on days when the Prime Minister was walking there. Janet's photo, taken as soon as she entered the park at about four-thirty, had been sent like all the others to Protection Command. The answer came back a few minutes later to all the phones of the security officers at the location: Janet Gradens was a person who had verbally abused the Prime Minister in February. She was unstable and should be watched closely. Two officers were ordered to pass by her to see if she was armed. Equipped with electronic metal detectors, while passing very close to her at about five o'clock, they had detected the knife, measured its shape and position in the jacket of her tracksuit. Control then sent instructions: "We won't arrest someone for having a kitchen knife but stop her from approaching the Prime Minister. If she comes near, immobilise her." The instructions had been executed to the letter by the man with the dog.

Surrounded by the six officers who formed a wall around her, Tracy was rushed to The Mall, about fifty yards away. While walking away, trying to see between the men, she noticed several snipers in position, covering the perimeter. The park was rapidly evacuated. She suddenly understood the extent of the resources mobilised for her walks, which no one had ever spoken to her about. When she got to The Mall, she was put in an armoured car which went straight to Downing Street. She was alone on a grey back seat, separated from the driver by a closed window. She wanted to understand what had happened, who this woman was who had just fainted and whom she had seen the police carry away. It was not until she arrived in her office that the Head of Security came to see her. He talked her through how the operation had unfolded. They couldn't have known if the jogger was going to stab her, but they couldn't take the risk. The woman had reached into her pocket within two yards of the Prime Minister. Officer B, who was accompanied by a dog, had intervened. Tracy asked a lot of questions about how her security was organised. She asked to congratulate Officer B, as well as the other police officers present. The Head of Security replied that her congratulations would be passed on, but the officers would not come to Downing Street to preserve their anonymity.

Meanwhile Janet Gradens woke up in the medical unit of a police station, shocked and dazed. She thought she had been dreaming. Only later, when the police questioned her, was she sure that she hadn't been hallucinating. Keeping her head down, eyes haggard, she kept up her initial story for a long time: she had bought a kitchen knife and carried it in her pocket on her way home. Late in the evening, however, she was questioned by the skilled psychologist who had already dealt with her on February 25th. She finally admitted that she had thought of killing Mrs Meller, whom she hated. She added, though, that at the last moment she had given up the idea. She had never taken the knife out of her pocket. The police did not extend her custody. They had no way of proving that Janet would have really done it. They needed to carry out a more detailed investigation. Meanwhile, the psychologist, having diagnosed the signs of a deep depression, decided to refer the young woman to a mental health clinic for treatment, under surveillance.

The case was reported in the media as an attempted attack on the Prime Minister by a mentally ill person. Janet Gradens' name, kept secret by the security services, did not appear. Some passers-by, who had filmed the scene on their mobile phones, including Janet's arrest and the Prime Minister's evacuation, discovered that their videos had been scrambled, and become unwatchable. Guy Wick made use of the incident, not hesitating to call it a "dangerous turn of the anti-Brexit movement". The matter was soon forgotten, when it was established that the woman who had attempted to commit the attack had acted alone, that she was suffering from severe depression, and that it was not clear whether she would have carried it through.

Tracy became psychologically affected a few days after the event. Initially, although she had wanted to congratulate the security detail for their dedication, she had considered the incident to be minor and the police response rather disproportionate. But, gradually, the idea that a person armed with a knife had wanted to stab her began to obsess her. She thought about it more and more and even had nightmares. What bothered her was not the risk to herself, because she was not fearful by nature. That she could inspire such hatred, however, disturbed her deeply. Was her policy so loathsome? Had she failed miserably? Her country was more divided than ever, the economy had plunged into a terrible crisis, the political situation was getting worse, her popularity rating was at its lowest ever, and now a violent attack: was this the sum total of her government's record? Was that what history would remember?

The Scottish Question

Just when it seemed to Tracy that things could hardly get any worse, the Scottish Parliament voted in favour of a new independence referendum. The question had caused deep divisions in the Scottish political scene since the Brexit vote on June 23rd, 2016. From the moment the results were in, the nationalists had stated that they wanted to stay in Europe and did not want to be dragged out by an English vote that was contrary to the wishes of most of the Scottish people. Progress had lagged after that, however. The independence movement faced considerable technical problems. Scotland's strong economic ties with England, the impossibility of balancing a budget with the oil price continuing low, the many practical obstacles made the project difficult to implement. Scottish public opinion, having voted 55% against independence in the 2014 referendum granted by David Cameron, remained divided. The pro-independence politicians did not want to risk another failure, which would stop their project in its tracks for a long time. They had decided to wait for a more favourable situation. In the 2018 General Election, the Conservative Party, in favour of keeping Scotland in Great Britain, had campaigned effectively. Scottish Conservatives did not see the same landslide results as the rest of the country but gained enough seats to diminish the influence of the Scottish National Party, which hampered the independence movement. Public opinion only began to change a good year later, starting in late 2019, when the UK's economic difficulties became increasingly obvious. Pro-independence voices began to speak up again. But the party did not have a majority and would have needed the support of the Scottish Labour MPs. Over the course of 2020, Jeremy Jones, newly appointed leader of the Labour Party, convinced his colleagues not to provide this support: the best strategy was to aim for victory in the next General Election, which Labour was almost certain to win. The United Kingdom would re-join Europe in the wake of the election, either by returning to the European Union or at least by joining the European Economic Area. It would be better to stay in the union and benefit from this return to Europe, than to embark on a risky independence project. This position stymied the Holyrood parliamentary debates on the subject again. By 2021, however, public opinion could no longer be ignored. Economic problems were on the rise, and people were openly blaming London's policy. It was time for Scotland to take its destiny into its own hands. The Scottish National Party won a landslide victory in the May 2021 Scottish parliamentary elections. The following months were devoted to constant debates and preparatory work. On 29th June 2022, in a historic vote, the Scottish Parliament finally voted for a new independence referendum to be held before June 2023, with a deadline permitting detailed plans to be drawn up. Polls the next day suggested the yes vote would be the winner with 65%. The date chosen was immediately criticised by London political circles: it virtually coincided with the British General Election, which would have to take place at the latest by the beginning of May 2023. But that was precisely what the nationalists were aiming for: they wanted the referendum to be held in the wake of the national election, to be won in the same spirit.

* * *

Tracy received the news of the Scottish decision with visible displeasure. The vote didn't surprise her, as the issue had been brewing for several months, but it was another blow for the country and one more problem to manage, which could bring down the stock market and the economy again just when markets had stabilised in June.

Technically the Scottish Parliament did not have the power to decide on a legally binding referendum, as constitutional matters were reserved for the Westminster Parliament. Without London's agreement, a Scottish referendum would be a mere consultation without legal force. In 2014, the vote had been approved by the London authorities, duly sanctioned by the Queen.

One of the reasons for the Prime Minister's irritation was that the Scottish Parliament's decision made no reference to an application for approval to the British Parliament. It was as if the Scots had decided that they could act unilaterally or as if agreement from Westminster were only a formality. Tracy had no intention of making things easier for them, but she was caught between two difficult choices: either she authorised the referendum, with the very high risk of the country splitting, given the economic situation and the results of the polls; or she blocked the referendum, which would enrage Scotland, where public feeling was now running very high. There would be demonstrations, maybe even riots. Given the series of unfortunate events Britain was going through at the moment, neither of the two scenarios was desirable.

She immediately telephoned the First Minister of the Scottish Parliament, to talk to her about the problem that this posed for the country, without kidding herself about the likely outcome of the conversation. The First Minister claimed the vote was triggered by "irresponsible policies led by London, which forced Scotland to take its destiny in hand" and refused to ask her Parliament to go back on its decision. Tracy replied that she had not decided to agree to the referendum and that was the end of their discussion.

The Prime Minister needed to give some deep thought to what to do next. Shaken by a barrage of bad news, rocked in her core convictions, she felt that she needed to meet with people who were experienced, and sure of their own beliefs. People who never let themselves be defeated by their circumstances. The two persons who best fitted this definition were, by a curious turn of fate, her worst political enemies. Guy Wick, for all his faults, was a strong politician. Nothing seemed to shake him. Every new event was data to be fed immediately into a succession of calculations, dissected, and analysed without prejudice, to produce the result which would be the most favourable outcome for his political ambitions. His first electoral defeat, when he was 23, as he tried to contest a constituency held by Labour for decades, was a textbook case. It could have put him off politics forever. The campaign had been tough, full of low blows, and the result had been humiliating for him. He had ended up in debt, his family and his party colleagues had advised him to pursue his career as a lawyer instead. Rather than following their advice, he spent the next few weeks on a detailed analysis of what he had missed, the wrong answers he had given during the debates, the technical subjects he had not dealt with well enough. Above all, instead of looking for work in London, he remained in the constituency, devoting the five years of the subsequent Parliament to accurately recording every mistake made by the Labour MP. He recorded voter complaints, made a note of which files were ignored, drew a diagram of the social movements in the constituency and the personal ambitions of the union and political leaders; he carefully recorded the weaknesses of the sitting MP, his expenses, and the associations that might be damaging to him when the time came; he had him followed by reliable friends. Five years later, after successfully persuading the Conservative Party to let him run again and his father to fund a new campaign, Guy Wick carried out an election campaign that turned into a textbook execution of the Labour candidate. The result was humiliating again, but this time for the other side. Guy Wick became one of the youngest members of Parliament and began the career that he was still pursuing. Every difficulty he encountered was treated with the same systematic energy. Having since inherited his father's fortune, Guy Wick now possessed significant financial resources, allowing him to devote all his energy to political action.

The other person Tracy thought of was Jeremy Jones. Very different from Guy Wick, diametrically opposed to him in his political choices and his methods, Jeremy Jones was a man who relied on instinct, who treated each subject with passion and conviction. He had discovered politics rather late in life and could have been put off by the low blows and difficulties in getting results. But nothing got to him: he was always on the move, he got up after each knockback and went back to the fight, wearing out his opponents one by one.

Tracy made an unprecedented decision: she invited Jeremy Jones and Guy Wick to Chequers for the following Saturday, the former to lunch, the latter to dinner. She certainly did not want them to meet each other. But these two very different heads might be just what she needed for brainstorming. She knew that both men were fiercely opposed to Scottish independence. On that front, they would be on her side. They would give her some arguments. Perhaps she could convince them to act with her for the good of the country.

When she contacted them personally, the two men accepted the invitation. No doubt they also wanted to size up the Prime

Minister before all the summer campaigns kicked off. Jones was due at twelve thirty, alone. He would leave at half past three. Wick would arrive in his Rolls-Royce, driven by his personal chauffeur, at six o'clock. The meetings would remain secret.

More meetings at Chequers

Saturday arrived quickly. Tracy had spent the rest of the week consulting with her ministers, as well as Philip Denniel, on strategies following the vote in the Scottish Parliament. She had made a statement on Friday outside Number 10, clearly laying out the risks posed to the country by another Scottish independence referendum. She had avoided saying whether she would block the process or whether she would seek the agreement of the British Parliament to approve it. She had left Downing Street on Friday night, happy to be able to spend a weekend at Chequers.

Jeremy Jones arrived, driving his own car, at the appointed hour. Despite their almost weekly clashes in Parliament, Tracy felt affectionately towards this jovial and direct man. They had never had lunch together, but she knew that conversation in the relaxed atmosphere of her country house would be easy.

Jones wasted no time.

"Scotland wants the same thing from the UK as you did from Europe," was the first thing he said as he jumped out of his car. "They want to leave our Union because they believe they will do better on their own. It's a fantasy. They should aim not to leave the Union, but to reform it. And that's what you should have done with the European Union."

"We go back 40 years with the European Union. The political union with Scotland goes back centuries. They aren't comparable," said Tracy, smiling as she held out her hand.

She took Jeremy Jones to the terrace where she offered him an aperitif. The weather was lovely on this first Saturday of July, and even quite hot already in the sun. They sat on wicker chairs brought out by the butler, under parasols. Jones had a whisky with two ice cubes, Tracy a cold lemonade. The Labour leader, who had come in summer clothes and wore a red t-shirt, remarked that it was good to enjoy the countryside in the summer. Then he returned to politics:

"I will not let this referendum take place. My party will oppose it in Parliament. Since your party will vote against it as well, the project will not be able to proceed."

"I agree," replied Tracy. "But how can we ignore the wishes of millions of the Scottish people? How will they react to what they will see as a denial of their democratic rights?"

"We will have to explain it to them. I will schedule several visits to Scotland in the coming months. I will tell them that their real opportunity is to be part of both Great Britain and Europe. I will convince them to vote for our party, so we can solve the problems they are facing. London and Brussels must contribute to Scotland's development. Human societies progress through solidarity, not isolationism."

"Solidarity is necessary, but it cannot be used as a policy or a cover for standardisation. Each country must develop its unique qualities. If the Union is such that it prevents countries from making the decisions that are necessary for them, they are better off independent."

"You see the contradictions of your party line, madam: you can't use the same arguments to explain that the United Kingdom must be outside the European Union and that Scotland must remain within the United Kingdom. This referendum will pose an insurmountable political problem. To my party, on the other hand, it quite naturally offers the opportunity of developing our proposed solution: a return to our historic unions, favourable to the economy and to social progress, and a simultaneous policy of solidarity and active government interventionism. This is the opposite of your closed-door policy."

"Edinburgh and London can work together, Mr Jones. The union of the United Kingdom is not comparable to membership of an organisation of twenty-eight countries with different economic and political histories and cultures. Our party's project is not 'every man for himself', it is 'everyone should govern at the most efficient level'. For Scotland, the devolution model gives all the flexibility required for local issues, while retaining the subjects that guarantee the union at the national level. An independent Scotland would lose on both counts: on the one hand it would no longer benefit from the advantages of its alliance with Great Britain; on the other hand by joining Europe as the Scottish National Party plans, it would no longer have the flexible decision-making process which it needs for local issues."

"Joining Europe would re-open the doors of the most active market in the world," replied Jones. "The country would also benefit from the weight of the EU in international negotiations. Without the European Union, we are dwarves in today's world and will be even more so in tomorrow's. Your policy has taken that opportunity away from the UK and it is natural that Scotland will not accept the outcome. For Scotland to stay in the UK, we need to change the perspective. You cannot have both Brexit and the integrity of the United Kingdom, Mrs Meller. You must make a choice: either you prioritise the unity of the nation and you will have to accept a compromise with the Scots on belonging to

Europe; or you carry on with Brexit, and sooner or later you will lose Scotland. We cannot prevent the referendum indefinitely."

Tracy did not want to reply to the dilemma Jones had outlined, a dilemma whose difficulty she felt all too keenly. Preferring to focus the discussion on how to prevent the referendum without appearing to be undemocratic, she invited Jeremy Jones to move into the dining room for lunch.

The Labour leader explained his programme of visits to Scotland, which he had decided on after the announcement of the Scottish Parliament's vote. He planned to visit the main cities and constituencies, meet people, and make a great many speeches. Of course, this plan allowed him to work on two fronts: he was also preparing the ground for the national General Election of 2023, as a better performance in Scotland would be necessary for a real victory at the national level. He would have to take a stance diametrically opposing that of the Scottish National Party.

This plan suited Tracy. Obviously, her party would also be looking to gain seats in Scotland, but her primary interest was in reducing the influence of the pro-independence SNP. She agreed with Jeremy Jones that in the meantime the question of the Scottish referendum should be submitted to the Westminster Parliament. The outcome of the debate, which would probably take place in October, was not in doubt: Parliament would reject the referendum request since both the Conservatives and Labour were against it. They would expect strong reactions from Scottish public opinion. The Prime Minister hoped that Jones' actions would mitigate them, but she could not agree with the Labour leader's unconditionally European line. The lunch ended without resolution on this point.

Tracy suggested that they have coffee in the Orangery by the indoor pool. After they had settled down and drunk their coffee, Jeremy Jones asked his host for a file and a plane. If she was surprised, she didn't show it.

"Certainly," she replied. "I'll ask the butler."

The tools were delivered promptly. The Prime Minister and the Chequers butler then witnessed the spectacle of the Leader of Her Majesty's Opposition, who faced down the government boldly every week during parliamentary sessions, effortlessly removing a French window door from the official residence, adjusting the edge with the plane, filing it down neatly, and rehanging the door. Jeremy Jones got to his feet, somewhat red in the face, and said, "I noticed that this French window was not closing properly. There was a risk of water getting in. All you have to do now is give it a lick of paint."

Returning the tools to the butler, he added: "I'll never forget I used to be a carpenter."

With that, he said goodbye to the Prime Minister, thanking her for the kind invitation. "Don't let Scotland leave the union," was his parting shot as he went through the house to return to the main courtyard. He got into his car, waved, and left without wasting any time.

"Always on the go," thought Tracy, watching the car head off. "Things will not be so easy with tonight's guest."

Having a little time in hand before Guy Wick arrived, she decided to go for a swim in the pool. The water was cool because, in keeping with Margaret Thatcher's tradition, she only heated it occasionally, to reduce housekeeping costs. She was cautious about her official expenses, certainly not wanting a press campaign accusing the Prime Minister of living in luxury while the rest of the nation was suffering financially.

At six o'clock, when she had just finished her shower and blow-dry, she heard a car in the driveway. It had to be Guy Wick, whose quasi-military punctuality was well known. Going down to the front lawn, she saw that it was indeed Wick's Rolls-Royce, tyres squealing on the front drive, coming around the central flowerbed to stop exactly in front of the entrance. The driver, wearing a top hat, got out to open the rear door. The prime minister saw first one foot emerge then the other. "Shoes from Foster & Son," she thought, aware of Wick's usual style of attire. Foster & Son, 83 Jermyn Street, was one of London's best-known luxury shoe manufacturers. Founded in 1840, the firm made bespoke shoes, fitted perfectly to the shape of each customer's foot, with a wait of some eight months. The financial crisis had not touched this renowned establishment; on the contrary, orders kept flooding in from around the world, encouraged by the pound's fall in value. Guy Wick shopped at Foster & Son not only out of personal taste, but also for the symbol of British success that this house represented. Above the well-shod feet, grey suit trousers with thin white stripes. "And that would be a suit from Anderson & Sheppard," thought Tracy, who was equally aware of the tailors, located at 32 Old Burlington Street, which had been dressing famous people since 1906. She then saw a mahogany cane sinking into the gravel of the yard, held on its golden pommel by a short hand with thick fingers. "I must find out where the cane comes from," thought Tracy. Guy Wick, up till then hidden in the depths of the car, finally emerged from the Rolls, and stood in front of Tracy, slightly shorter than her, wearing a hat to shade his oval face, proudly wearing the impeccable suit which attempted to conceal his girth, and with a serious expression on his face. Despite her dislike for Guy Wick, Tracy could not help smiling inside. "They don't make them like they used to. A three-piece suit for the countryside on a hot summer's day. He looks as if he has just stepped out of one of the members' clubs in St James."

"The drive is magnificent," were Guy Wick's first words. "But the beeches planted by Winston Churchill are suffering. The leaves have weevils. You should have them treated."

"I know," replied Tracy, "Chequers' gardeners are aware of the problem and are administering the correct treatment."

She had seen the attack coming. Talking about the beech trees planted by Churchill was a way of reminding her that she had been preceded at Chequers by more prestigious Prime Ministers than her, while pointing out that she was neglecting their legacy by allowing the trees to deteriorate. It could only be a previously planned attack, because those beeches were not on the usual route in taken by visitors.

"Do let's hope your gardeners are successful," said Wick. "There are enough things going wrong in the country at present."

Hearing this new critical remark, Tracy was tempted to propose to the Conservative party grandee that they go for a walk in the sun, still hot even now, just for the pleasure of making him sweat in his suit. But her good manners, and the respect she had for Foster & Son shoes as well as for Anderson & Sheppard suits, held her back and she took her guest for an aperitif in the Great Hall. The conversation quickly turned to the Scottish referendum. Although they were colleagues in the same party, and had known each other for years, these two politicians were not on first name terms.

"Scotland wants to leave the UK because the economic situation is dire," Guy Wick stated. "We must prevent this vote until the situation has stabilised. When it has, they will choose the path of reason, like in 2014. It is much more in Scotland's interests to stay in the United Kingdom rather than setting off on the path to independence. In addition, the last vote was barely eight years ago. We cannot keep voting so often on a constitutional subject of such importance, which has implications for generations to come. You must strongly oppose this vote."

"What public position will you take?" asked Tracy.

She could see Guy Wick's game quite clearly: the Scottish referendum was an opportunity for him to speak out about the country's economic situation, in effect, to criticise her, while letting her shoulder the responsibility for refusing the referendum. So it was important to know if she would have any support on the issue.

"I'll say people have the right to choose their future," said Wick. "But that the time is not right for a referendum, because of the economic difficulties the country is going through. I will leave it to the government to agree on a more appropriate date with the Scottish Parliament."

"Will you go to Scotland as part of the series of engagements you have planned for the summer?"

"Yes, but I will not be changing my itinerary or the content of my speeches. I want to mobilise people who are in favour of going forward with Brexit, as you know. So I will be talking about the situation the country is in, and the measures which need to be taken."

Tracy had her answer. What a difference from Jeremy Jones! The Labour leader had immediately proposed taking on a part of the struggle, by going to Scotland to convince his counterparts to change strategy. Guy Wick, meanwhile, was just carrying on with his plan to conquer the government, was not going to take any risks on the referendum and would be ready to take advantage of the difficulties it would cause her.

Dinner was announced and served soon after this conversation. Guy Wick spent the meal telling Tracy that the country needed an urgent change in government policy.

"We will not solve our economic problems by continuing on with the current policy. You take too much notice of economists, and Denniel in particular. We must stop trying to cushion the blow for the sectors that are not coming out of recession. Let them reform themselves, and let us support those who are successful. And you hesitate too much: one day you're all for Brexit, the next in favour of opening discussions with Europe. I know what meetings you have scheduled at the G20 summit next week. With this attitude, you will add further uncertainty to an already very difficult political situation."

"I have to explore all the options that could benefit the country," said Tracy. "As for the economic choices, I don't think you have the measure of the scale of the work undertaken by the government team, under the Chancellor's leadership, and with the support of the Bank of England, to prevent the crisis from becoming even more serious."

"I will tell you what's behind my reasoning, madam. The country, rocked by the current crisis, is facing three major risks. Firstly, throwing itself into the arms of Labour in the next election, who will implement a costly government spending programme that our economy cannot support; the second would be following Jones' proposal to return to Europe, that is, to again become part of a bureaucratic organisation that will block its decision-making capabilities; finally, a break-up of the country if the Scots get their vote, which will be the case if we don't take serious action. I believe that, faced with these issues, the Conservative Party has to go into the next election with a very strong manifesto. You led the party to victory in 2018, brilliantly. In 2023 it's going to take a leader able to lead just as well, with strength and unity. I think you are no longer in a position to do that, after the wear and tear of the last five years. I propose to take on that role, becoming the leader of the party towards the end of this year."

Tracy bit back her immediate response to this challenge.

"The leader of the party for the next election will be selected according to our usual rules, Mr Wick. You know as well as I that it is not down to us to come to an arrangement on this subject.

MORE MEETINGS AT CHEQUERS

As far as I am concerned, I am determined to serve my country as long as I have the confidence of Parliament."

Unwilling to pursue the conversation on this topic, she invited her guest to have coffee in the Great Hall. Once comfortably seated in a leather chair, Guy Wick lit a cigar, having received a nod of assent from Tracy. The atmosphere relaxed a little.

"I have an abiding passion for this country," Wick explained. "Great Britain is not great only in name, but from its history, its influence on the world, its civilisation which continues to inspire so many nations. I will never accept this country going into a decline. It can undergo trials, as has been the case in the past and as is happening at the moment. But our people are still standing. And if I have to make difficult choices for the good of our nation, I will. Europe, globalisation, the huge influx of foreigners, were distorting the very nature of our country. We have undertaken Brexit to put an end to this wrong turn. Holding to this course is sometimes painful, but necessary. You must not change it."

"We will have to accept some adaptations, Mr Wick. It is not a matter of putting our sovereignty on the line, but of clear-sightedly putting right what didn't work from the choices we made."

"That's where our difference of opinion lies," said Wick. "I am convinced that with certain policy tweaks, Brexit will achieve the success we dreamed of in future. In the meantime, I will not change course."

The political conversation concluded with this remark. The Prime Minister and her guest began to discuss the history of Chequers, which they both knew well and enjoyed exchanging stories about. Guy Wick expressed a desire to see Lady Mary Grey's room, so they went upstairs. They saw the inscription that the girl had left on a wall. Guy Wick also spent some time in the Long Gallery, where he examined Cromwell's death mask. Returning to the Great Hall with his hostess, he went to the piano and played several pieces by Gustav Holst. At the end of the evening, as he was preparing to leave, Tracy got round to the question she had wanted to ask from the start.

"I recognised where your suit and shoes came from," she said. "But where did you get your cane?"

Guy Wick did not answer right away. He blushed a little. Then he said: "It's from Fayet, a French company. Many well-known people shop there, and they have even supplied the Japanese imperial family."

Tracy laughed up her sleeve at Wick's passing discomfort. The staunch defender of Brexit XXL, Mr "100% British", was a little ashamed to admit that he sometimes bought French goods, however prestigious they were.

Guy Wick's campaign

The senior Conservative politician undertook his summer programme as planned. He organised his first meeting in Dudley, in the heart of the Black Country, one of the centres of the British Industrial Revolution.

The origin of the term "Black Country", anecdotally seems to be related either to the abundance of coal deposits, with large seams lying close to the surface, or to the pollution which covered the area with soot in the Victorian era. Guy Wick's choice was far from random: Dudley had been selected for its symbolic importance, because of its history, both remote and recent.

Mining operations and metal working in the area date back to at least the Middle Ages. The town of Dudley was already important in the eleventh century and a castle was built after the Norman conquest. The town centre was home to a famous market, and exported iron items throughout the country. In the seventeenth century Colonel Dud Dudley invented a method of using coal instead of charcoal for iron manufacture. This earned him the wrath of the charcoal burners, who destroyed his furnaces. The invention did not make his fortune. But the idea was taken up and coal proved to be a much more abundant resource than charcoal. The first steam engines appeared at the beginning of the following century. Technical innovation, increasing use of coal, and the construction of canals to facilitate transportation led to a very rapid expansion in industry. In addition to coal mining, metalworking, and limestone quarrying, other industries such as machinery, glass and textiles sprang up. The region became one of the hearts of the Industrial Revolution.

The cost of this, unfortunately, was the suffering of the workers, both adults and children. There were not only desperate working conditions, but severe pollution. Dudley was described in 1852 in a government report as "the most unhealthy place in the country". A tour guide written at the time by Samuel Sidney, Rides on Railways, described the dim light during the day, the incandescence of the factory chimneys that lit up the night, and the general pollution. "The pleasant green of pastures is almost unknown, the streams, in which no fishes swim, are black and unwholesome." We do not know if this description encouraged ticket sales for the railway company, the London and North Western Railway ... especially as the guide went on to describe the inhabitants as "savages, without the grace of savages, coarsely clad in filthy garments (...) they converse in a language belarded with fearful and disgusting oaths, which can scarcely be recognised as the same as that of civilised England." Like a modern Moloch, the Industrial Revolution, which was to transform the whole world, burned and crushed in its heart the poor creatures who fed its fires, without the slightest gratitude from the upper classes in London. The harsh working conditions led to one of the biggest strikes in the country's history in 1913.

After suffering from industrialisation, the region experienced the woes of de-industrialisation. The decline of the coal industry in the twentieth century hit the local economy hard. The last mine in the Black Country closed in 1968. This led to high levels of unemployment, worsened by the liberal restructuring of the

1980s. Shops gradually disappeared from the centre of Dudley, preferring to relocate to a large newly-created out of town shopping centre. Great redevelopment plans were undertaken, especially in the service sector, with definite successes, a sign of the courage and tenacity of the inhabitants. But in the early 2010s, according to a government report, the area was still significantly lagging behind.

In spite of all these difficulties, the locals have a deep pride in their region and show no desire to leave. They also love their country and have committed beliefs. The Dudley constituency Brexit vote had the largest lead in the polls in June 2016: 118,446 votes for Brexit, 56,780 votes against. The wider West Midlands region voted by more than 59% to leave the European Union, and Dudley more than 67%, while the national result was slightly below 52%. The 2018 General Election confirmed this trend, with the Conservative Party winning a clear majority with its Brexit XXL programme.

Guy Wick had chosen Dudley for the first meeting of his campaign, both for its industrial past, which he wanted to highlight, and for its pro-Brexit beliefs. As the town was only small, it would not be a large gathering but effectively a symbolic launch intended to mobilise his supporters.

That evening, the meeting hall was full and the atmosphere very excited even before the arrival of the Conservative politician. Most of the audience was made up of workers, employees, pensioners, and the unemployed. A lot of people were worried, even desperate. Jeremy Jones, a former manual worker, would have felt closer to this audience than Guy Wick, who was worth tens of millions of pounds. But Labour, who had held the town for a very long time, had felt unconvincing for the voters for some years now. The Conservatives had taken the Dudley South constituency in 2010 and still held it. In Dudley North, the other constituency, UKIP had gradually been taking more and more votes from Labour, but in 2018, it was the Conservative candidate, with his Brexit XXL campaign, who had toppled the incumbent Labour MP.

Guy Wick was always comfortable with a crowd. He prepared all his appearances very thoroughly and knew how to play on his natural charisma. He had already visited Dudley twice and was known there. Today, he had organized a free buffet for all the meeting attendees, with burgers, sausages, fish and chips, and as much beer as you liked, which had boosted his public appeal no end. He was believed, with good reason, to be a strong personality: someone who was not afraid of his convictions, who didn't waffle, and who had a plan for the country. People liked that; many wanted to hear him tonight to find out what he was going to set out.

He arrived at about six-thirty, by coach from Birmingham (no Rolls-Royce for campaign meetings ... but he still wore the three-piece suit). He began by having a beer at the buffet and chatting with the attendees. Many people were flattered that Wick had chosen Dudley as the first stop on his new campaign. Everyone was talking about an assault at lunchtime in Birmingham, which had been widely featured on the news. Young visiting students had attacked some workers after a political debate during which the latter had declared their opposition to any return to the European Union. The youths had insulted the workers, then began attacking them with bats, before fleeing the scene when the police arrived. This scenario, identical to what had happened on June 25th, had been profoundly shocking for the viewers. That evening in Dudley, they were waiting to hear Guy Wick's position on this violent provocation. The press was covering the meeting, which would give his speech a national impact.

At half-past seven, Wick climbed onto the platform and grabbed the microphone.

"My friends, for weeks now Jeremy Jones' supporters have been trying, through street protests, and now by violence, to impose their idea of a return to the European Union. I am saying right now that it has to stop!"

Shouts of agreement broke out round the hall. Guy Wick continued:

"This kind of contempt for our democratic process is unacceptable! The people of this country have – twice! – voted for a clear mandate to leave the European Union. And you, Dudley, were the leaders of the movement, making your voice heard with your votes, the best result in the whole country!"

More shouts and applause from the audience.

"And now, your voice is being ignored! Tell me, how many times has Jeremy Jones come to see you over the last two years that he's been Labour leader?"

"None!" shouted out the crowd, as one.

"Absolutely. He hasn't come. Because Jeremy Jones doesn't waste time with people who don't think like him. He wants to impose his views, his choices, on everyone in England."

The crowd booed Jeremy Jones. Guy Wick continued:

"We are told that Brexit has caused an economic crisis. Weren't there economic crises before Brexit? Have they forgotten 2008-2009? Have they forgotten the years of de-industrialisation too? Dudley, more than any other area perhaps, has lived it. These difficulties were a result of globalisation, the madness of our economy competing with countries that do not have the same social standards. And who pushed us in that direction? Who, if it wasn't Europe?"

Boos for Europe. Guy Wick continued:

"Today's crisis, friends, comes from a different source. Our country is being targeted by speculators! The banks never wanted Brexit, they won't stop fighting for a return to the open market, a good option – for them. As they have failed to convince the government, the big financial players are bringing down stock market prices to achieve their ends. When the country has its back to the wall, the government will have to give in and renegotiate an agreement with Europe. I am saying right now that we must not give in to this blackmail! I'm saying that we must put a stop to these stock market machinations! And I'm saying that government money, instead of being used to save the banks, should be used to support our industry!"

Applause and cries of approval in the hall.

"Your region, like our whole country, is rich with resources! Our industry, which was the first in the world, can flourish again if we protect and support it. Leaving Europe allows us to take these protective measures because we are free to make our own decisions. Dudley, like the rest of the country, can get back real industrial jobs. But for that to happen, it's vital that the British people don't follow Jeremy Jones. If we go back into the European Union, or even the European Economic Area, we will be re-entrenched in a system of twenty-eight country decision-making, a system that has to take into account each country's priorities. But our priority, my friends, is Great Britain! What this government has not managed to do yet, will be achieved in the next Parliament. Once the speculators are defeated, we will realign our policy to support industry. That's when the full success of our country will be obvious to everyone."

This prospect launched new applause.

"But in the meantime, my friends, we cannot let thugs attack us. Can you imagine if they came here to Dudley with more of this kind of violence, because your town doesn't vote the way they want?"

"Let'em come!" a voice shouted out. "We'll be ready for them!"

"Quite right," said Wick. "And there's even more that you can do! We've had enough of Jeremy Jones taking centre stage with his demonstrations. We will show the country that Leavers are still in the majority. We are going to prove the polls wrong! I'm inviting you all to a gigantic demonstration on September 24th! We will gather in all the major cities right across the country – especially Birmingham! And we will remind everyone that our voices count, and that we will not let ourselves be attacked! See you on September 24th, my friends! Our country needs your support! Dudley has to send another clear message out to the whole nation!"

The hall cheered Wick's speech. A lot of people shouted that they would be there on September 24th. Wick came down from the platform and mingled with the crowd. The evening was a success, which the media would broadcast throughout the country.

Guy Wick was already thinking about the next meeting in Birmingham. The audience would be different, a more mixed crowd with not all so favourable to his thinking. The city was one of the few English cities that had voted in favour of Brexit, but only with a narrow majority. Six years later, opinions had changed, and anti-Brexiteers were now in the majority. Guy Wick needed to create a sense of urgency among his supporters: galvanising them was essential to prevent the country from changing direction.

September Divisions

The demonstrations on 17th and 24th September 2022 were some of the largest the country had ever seen. The first, organized by Jeremy Jones, brought together two million people in twenty different cities. The Labour leader had spent all summer preparing for the event, which was to be the culmination of the movement he had started in February. From October, preparations for the 2023 general election would take priority over all other activities and there would be no point in demonstrating for the government's resignation a few months before an election. So Jones was counting on September 17th to be a last show of strength that would be useful for him at the launch of the election campaign. An intensive campaign over several weeks prepared supporters for the event, and the crowd went en masse to different meeting points on the day, despite the showery weather. Participants were particularly exasperated by how the national situation had deteriorated since the February crisis and by what they saw as the government's stubbornness in refusing to change its political line. Jeremy Jones had decided to hold his demonstration in Hyde Park to mirror the one at the beginning of his campaign. There were well over a million people there for his speech. Holograms representing him relayed the speech in real time in all the cities where rallies were taking place. He reiterated his usual themes of the need to return to a social policy backed by a renewed membership of the European market. He discussed the idea of a "flexible Union", as several European leaders were now terming it. According to him, the United Kingdom should rejoin the European market as soon as possible, whether the Union had been transformed or not, but the flexible Union would offer an additional advantage, allowing the country to tailor its membership according to its own priorities. He went on to detail the measures he was proposing to take immediately to stimulate the economy, as well as the measures to be implemented to support the sectors of the population who were most affected by the current crisis.

With the massive success of his movement, Jones looked set to be Britain's next Prime Minister. He was more popular than ever, and his party was far ahead in the polls. Opposing him, Tracy Meller's approval rating was at its lowest ever, and the divisions within the Conservative Party were becoming more and more evident.

That didn't take into account, however, the extraordinary energy Guy Wick was demonstrating at the same time. After his rally in Dudley, the senior Conservative had spent the summer crisscrossing the country. He had brilliantly laid out his pro-Brexit ideas, while now distancing himself from the government's economic policy. He had convinced opponents of a return to the European Union of the necessity for urgent action. He had finally announced what everyone was waiting for: a big demonstration, a first for the pro-Brexit movement. He had raged against the unacceptable actions of anti-Brexit activists, who had caused outbreaks of violence again at the close of the demonstration on the 17th. On September 24th, across cities carefully selected by him, one and a half million people rallied to refuse any compromise on the independence of Great Britain. Attendance, although half a million fewer people than at

Jones' demonstrations, was massive and indicated the continuing underlying support of a significant part of the country for the policy of Brexit. Even if the line of majority opinion had probably changed sides, Britain remained deeply divided.

* * *

Tracy stayed in London for the two weekends of 17th and 24th September. As she worked in her office, she could hear slogans being chanted by protesters crossing Whitehall or St James's Park to the demonstrations. She watched the television broadcasts and saw the national divisions solidifying into two seemingly irreconcilable camps.

She had been very active all summer. Her meetings with political leaders on the sidelines of the G20 summit had paid off. The famous transitional provisions were about to be extended for another three years. The agreement, which would be announced at the end of September, would reassure the key economic players, and the foreign nationals worried about the extension of their residence permits. Tracy had also got carefully chosen members of her cabinet to start discreet discussions with several European countries on the outline plans for a flexible Union. The objective was to prepare proposals to be submitted in October to the Conservative Party conference, focusing on a return to the European Union while retaining the essential elements of sovereignty. This approach was extremely risky. Tracy knew Guy Wick and his movement had an unbending opposition to any proposal of this kind. The other wings of the party would be more receptive to the ideas, but the political balance would nevertheless remain extremely delicate: if Tracy did not obtain a majority at the conference, she would have to stand down; if she did win a majority, Guy Wick would cause a party split by leaving the Conservatives, taking at least a third of MPs with him, probably more: this scenario would also result in her fall, as she would no longer have a majority in the Commons. Guy Wick would form a new political movement alongside UKIP. Deprived of a significant part of their support base, the Conservatives would be defeated by Labour. Tracy had been turning these ideas over and over in her head for weeks without reaching any resolution. The success of Guy Wick's demonstration on September 24th highlighted the trickiest part of the situation: the Conservative challenger would feel strong enough to refuse any negotiation and it was even possible that a majority of Conservative MPs would join him.

On Monday, September 26th, late in the afternoon, two days after the Wick demonstration, Tracy was thinking in her office while looking down on the 10 Downing Street garden through the window. Further away, in St James's Park, the leaves of the trees had already taken on autumn colours. Someone knocked at the door. Tracy turned around and saw her secretary announcing the President of the Financial Club, slightly early for his appointment. The visitor was none other than James Callagher, the wealthy Chairman of HGB Bank. The Prime Minister asked him to come in.

The Financial Club, a private club for City leaders, was one of the most powerful lobbies in Britain. It was sometimes confused with UK Finance, the professional association of banks and financial institutions, although it was a completely separate entity. The Financial Club was effectively a lobbying group. Its power, diminished in recent years by the difficulties of some of its member establishments, remained considerable. The club had very large funds and an extensive network of Members of Parliament, both Conservative and Labour. Its political action had always been in favour of the European Union, supporting all the provisions which allowed British banks to operate freely on the continent, and which for so many years had ensured the tremendous success of the City of London. The club had vociferously opposed Brexit XXL, but its influence, limited to the ruling classes, could not prevent the electoral tidal wave, followed by Britain's unilateral exit from the Union.

Tracy had known James Callagher for years, although she was not particularly fond of him. Champion of an industrially strong Britain which would encourage the regions, based on an economic model benefiting the middle classes, Tracy had never been the City's preferred candidate. She was of the view that the banks had gained too much power since the 1980s and that the UK economy had become too reliant on London's financial sector. The influx of capital into London, certainly a source of jobs, had created a class of high-earners, led to rocketing property prices, and widened the gap with the less privileged regions. Londoners had mostly voted against Brexit, unlike the rest of England. Tracy agreed on this point with Guy Wick, supporter of a policy based primarily on industry and services. The senior Conservative was known for his mistrust of the City and regularly denounced the harmful influence of the banks in his speeches. His detractors attributed his attitude to the fact that the big banks had refused to bail his father out when he had experienced financial troubles in the 1980s.

More pragmatic than Wick, Tracy still kept up good relations with the banks, aware of their vital role in the country's economy. She wondered, however, what Callagher had come to tell her.

She suggested to the President that they have their conversation in the small sitting room next to her office, where she would have tea served. After some discussion of recent events, Callagher came to the point of his visit.

"Prime Minister, we believe that our country is being offered an unprecedented political opportunity. The European Union is going to be reformed in a way that suits the wishes of the majority of our fellow citizens. Our club believes that Britain must seize this opportunity to return, through the front door, to a European Union that would benefit our strategic economic interests. It will be possible to do so without renouncing the essential components of our sovereignty, given the profound institutional changes that will be implemented by the EU. We think that your party, and you in particular, could offer the country that choice, thanks to this new European development, without reneging on the policies you have implemented since 2016. Mr Jones is certainly already proposing this as a plan. But our financial community does not want him in power: his social projects are extremely expensive and would be harmful to our economy. We would very much like you to be the standard bearer of this major political change. We know that you have begun to discuss this possibility with some members of your team and we understand that you are not opposed to it."

"I asked for a study of the proposals for institutional changes in Europe, so that our government will know how to respond to them if necessary. If these provisions are beneficial for our country, we will not hesitate to propose a Parliamentary inquiry."

Tracy answered without quite showing her hand, but she had said enough to satisfy the President. She continued:

"You know, however, Mr Callagher, that a sizeable wing of the Conservative Party is against a return, even with guarantees of sovereignty."

"That's exactly why I'm here, Prime Minister," the President said. "I came to tell you that if you went down this path, you would have the full support of our club. We would help to convince a good many of your MPs, many of whom are close to us as you know. We would also be able to reduce Mr Wick's influence," he added, looking the Prime Minister in the eye.

Tracy held his gaze, wondering just what Callagher meant by that, but he did not go into detail.

"I'm glad your club is in touch with our MPs," she said. "Links between members of Parliament and key players in the economy are essential. However, I would like to think that our MPs are independent and not under the influence of any kind of organisation. Besides, I don't remember your interventions being that effective in recent years."

Tracy still had in mind the numerous measures taken by the club in early 2018 to prevent Brexit XXL. Callagher had even come to Downing Street then, to no avail. Tracy had listened politely but ignored his warnings.

"You're right, madam, we could not prevent the political choices that were made at the time. We could not convince most of the members of your party, mainly because of the electoral situation. But we believe that the circumstances have changed and that it's time for us to act, with the means at our disposal. We have good reasons to believe that your MPs will be open to a new policy, and we will be happy to contribute to this discussion, without, of course, influencing their independence of action." (He did not add that Tracy Meller herself was listening to him today with considerably more attention than she had four years ago.)

"Some MPs will certainly be in favour. But Guy Wick got one and a half million protesters onto the streets, Mr Callagher. He's in no mood for making concessions."

"We are aware of that, madam. However, we think we have some convincing arguments."

As Callagher still refrained from providing any more details, Tracy understood that she would not find out anything more that day. She had picked up a hint that the means of influencing MPs would be financial: the MPs who chose the direction endorsed by the club would see, as if by magic, their electoral campaigns generously funded. She did not like that kind of method and knew that many MPs were irreproachable in that respect. But she was not unaware that these things were sometimes done in subtle ways, often invisible even to the candidates themselves. In any case she could not do anything at this stage. The Parliamentary standards committees would have to do their jobs. Against Wick, however, financial incentives would be no use, because he did not need the money. Callagher presumably had something else in mind, but Tracy could not guess what. She moved the conversation on to economic matters. The President assured her that if she announced a policy change the financial markets would recover dramatically. In addition, he hinted that certain larger banks could help undertake technical measures, in collaboration with the Bank of England, to improve the economic situation in the forthcoming months (i.e. in time for the elections): for example, they could grant loans much more easily, which would boost investment. Finally, they could intervene in the markets to support prices and push up sterling to lower the cost of imports.

"Your Chancellor is very supportive of these measures," said Callagher, looking at the Prime Minister.

Tracy instantly understood the President's allusion: if she did not take the tack he wanted, Callagher would try to bring her down and have the Chancellor – who would lead the desired campaign – elected in her place as party leader. "Another Wick, so calculating," she thought. "But with vastly greater financial resources... And he has the means to get rid of Wick, otherwise he would not be so confident." A frightening thought crossed her mind: was all this part of a much older plan? Could the February crash have been orchestrated by this diabolical businessman, to disrupt the economy and put the Conservative Party, and herself, under such pressure that renouncing Brexit would become the only possible path? She had always thought the market's reaction had been very excessive, difficult to justify rationally. Did Callagher control speculators like Luke Trosden, were they his straw men? But no, it wasn't possible, she thought, he would have to have had a considerable influence on other banks and financial institutions. And surely he would not have deliberately triggered events that would put his own bank in danger? She considered all these caveats but could not quite rid herself of the doubts that had taken hold of her. She remembered Wick had often said that the crisis was due to speculators. She looked at Callagher. He was drinking his tea impassively looking over at St. James's Park in the distance, just as she had been doing earlier. She had visited him once at Kensington Palace Gardens, in his home which alone was worth tens of millions of pounds. She knew that Callagher was a multibillionaire. "His personal means, not to mention those of the banks in the club, are obviously immense. He is certainly able to buy and influence people," she thought. She suddenly remembered that it was Callagher who had introduced her to Denniel almost three years ago and who had strongly recommended him as an excellent candidate to head the Bank of England. "Denniel's honesty is unimpeachable. But that does not preclude all contact. Maybe Callagher gives him advice? Or is Denniel Callagher's way of knowing what is going on in the bank and predicting its actions?"

Tracy shivered. Callagher looked at her, and she passed it off by saying that it was starting to get a little chilly now it was the end of September. Callagher nodded and said goodbye, reminding her of the need to make the right choice for the country. Tracy remained thoughtful after his departure. What was the real power of these financial institutions whose resources were in the hundreds of billions? The weaker ones, Merlin bank, the HGB bank, had cracked under the pressure of the crisis. But how many more, banks, pension funds, investment funds, both in Britain and abroad, still controlled fortunes? What did politicians count for in the face of the kind of power that could make and break markets? One thing was certain, however:

Callagher had come to see her. He still thought that she could lead the party to victory. The good relations she maintained with European leaders would be crucial if a plan for return to the EU were to be implemented. That probably explained his approach. In the short term, he needed her. In the medium term, however, he would surely like to have someone more malleable than her in the role of Prime Minister. He would bring her down when the time was right. Tracy shook her head.

"I've got to stop thinking about that. There's no proof of all these wild speculations." She decided to take a stroll in the garden to clear her head.

At the same moment, Callagher, leaving Downing Street, was getting into his limo. "We're going to see Jeremy Jones now," he announced to his driver.

Change of direction

On Wednesday, September 28th, in the late afternoon, the Prime Minister's car, driving along the Mall, passed a regiment of Horse Guards trotting on horseback, beautiful and impassive in the rain. Tracy was on her way to Buckingham Palace for her weekly meeting with the Queen. She looked at the riders, admiring their silver cuirasses. "What a difference from my visit in May 2018," she thought. That day, after her landslide victory in the election, she had been very emotional, surrounded by the same Horse Guards, as she went to Buckingham Palace to be confirmed as Prime Minister. Although she had been in office for two years already at that point, her initial appointment had only been as the result of an internal election within her party. This time she was invested with the full legitimacy of an undeniable electoral victory. She had travelled the same route to the palace, greeting the crowd, arriving dazzled by the flashes of the photographers. After going up the Grand Staircase and performing the obligatory curtesy to the Queen, the meeting with the sovereign had been very cordial and her appointment was confirmed with all due process. She had returned to Downing Street to make a speech full of hope for "the new era that was opening up for our nation". She had foreseen a few difficulties, the markets were already down and the economy showing signs of slowing, but she thought that all this was temporary, due to the uncertainties of the transition to Brexit. She had been more than ever convinced that a bright future was waiting for Britain. Moreover, none of the economists' pessimistic forecasts about Brexit had come true since the referendum. Few people would have bet on a recession the following year, such predictions as John Klin's having fallen on deaf ears.

Today, four years later, she was Prime Minister of a country in deep crisis, the people were suffering, her popularity was at an all-time low and her party members were just waiting for the right moment to bring her down.

She arrived in the courtyard of Buckingham Palace to the drum of heavy rain. Her umbrella, which was held by an assistant as she got out of the car, blew away in a gust of wind. She was relieved to enter the palace, where a peaceful calm reigned. When she reached the audience room, the sovereign, who was waiting for her with her usual courtesy, made no secret of her preoccupation with the state of the country, which was very divided after the huge demonstrations that month. Always very scrupulous in the remarks she addressed to the Prime Minister, taking care not to interfere in the current political affairs, Her Majesty could, however, be very direct: "You must restore the unity to the country. Please, bear this in mind as you consider your forthcoming decisions."

Tracy confirmed that the unity of the country was her primary concern and had always driven her actions. She acknowledged that the situation was critical, requiring strong decisions. She told the Queen about the initiatives she would be taking in the forthcoming days. After the meeting, she returned to Downing Street, still in the ministerial car because of the rain, determined to implement a completely new phase of her policy. The announcements she would make would take the country on a major change of course.

***

On Friday, September 30th, outside 10 Downing Street, the Prime Minister announced an extension of the transitional provisions for another three years, which had just been validated with the European Union. The news was hailed by public opinion and the markets. The stock market and the pound went up. After the weekend, at Tracy's instigation, the House of Commons, instead of voting for or against allowing a new Scottish independence referendum, decided to appoint a parliamentary commission which would "study the question in depth, would have detailed discussions with all the stakeholders and would make a full report to the House" (this was of course a way to delay the decision by several months). On Wednesday, 5th October, during Prime Minister's Question Time, Tracy recommended that Parliament "study the changes proposed to the European constitution by our partners in order to see if, in certain circumstances, these new provisions could be beneficial to Great Britain and could prompt a re-examination of the country's relations with Europe". She did not use the words "accession to a reformed European Union", but her statement had the effect of a political bombshell. Guy Wick was on his feet demanding to know if the Prime Minister intended to return to a policy of surrender of sovereignty. Tracy declared that this was certainly not her intention, but that it was her duty to study any course of action of potential benefit to Great Britain. In a theatrical gesture, Guy Wick stalked out of the Commons chamber. In the afternoon, he made a statement on television: "I believe that the Prime Minister is about to betray her commitment to the citizens who voted for our national independence. If this is confirmed, it will be our duty to oppose her action with the utmost firmness. I will ask the Conservative Party to commence proceedings to elect a new leader."

CHANGE OF DIRECTION

The Conservative party conference was to be held at the end of October, delayed by one month from its traditional date. Guy Wick had requested, and obtained, this change back in June, in order to better accommodate his own plans. It was the moment he was aiming to be elected to head the party in place of Tracy Meller, and so become Prime Minister. The Conservative politician no longer had any reason to hold back. He began his campaign at the weekend by viciously attacking Tracy in statements. He accused her of wanting to be "the gravedigger of British national identity after already burying its economy through her mismanagement". He said the crisis the country was going through was not due to Brexit, but to her incompetent decisions. He criticized her industrial policy and her failure to negotiate bilateral trade agreements, which had condemned the country to operate under the constraint of damaging customs barriers. He castigated her indolence in the face of attacks by those he called "the speculators of the financial markets, who feed on the ruin of others and want to bring the country to its knees". He called for the establishment of a policy of real business support to boost the economy, and explicitly asked the party to appoint a new leader at the conference.

The newspapers seized on the Meller-Wick battle, making predictions about the respective support that each of them would get inside the party. The first polls quickly revealed deep fault lines among Conservatives. One third of the members supported Tracy, on a pragmatic line: "Let's see what Europe is doing, and if that's good for us, we'll consider a rapprochement." Another third was lining up behind Wick, opposed to any return for Britain to "an unmanageable Union of twenty-eight countries, which will be even more complicated when it is multi-tier". The final third was torn between the two camps, undecided between the arguments of each side. Tracy, for her part, tried to clarify her proposals in several speeches. She was not proposing accession to the European Union, as this subject would have to be studied in detail when the outlines of the reforms to the Union were known, but she was encouraging the members of the party to "Open your eyes to the facts and take advantage of opportunities that could be good for the country".

In the days that followed, as the party conference drew nearer, it became clear that Guy Wick was rapidly gaining ground in the Conservative ranks. His attacks were hitting home. The shine was off Tracy's reputation after six years in power, not to mention the very awkward situation of her proposing a radical change when she had been championing a hard Brexit since 2018. Moreover, her position was still too vague to elicit passionate support, while Guy Wick was defending a well understood and longstanding policy. By October 15th, polls on the voting intentions of party members showed Wick ahead, with his lead growing daily. The country was preparing to have a Prime Minister from the most hard-line pro-Brexit camp. Jeremy Jones, who had left the Conservatives to tear each other apart, took the opportunity to rally everyone who "has had enough of a party that is driving the country over a cliff".

★ ★ ★

On the evening of Sunday, October 23rd, less than a week before the party conference, while the Prime Minister was in her office at 10 Downing Street preparing for her next day's meetings, an urgent note was brought to her from the Home Secretary: "It appears Guy Wick was the instigator of the violence in the summer." Stunned, Tracy scanned the text from a police report clearly incriminating the senior Conservative figure. Apparently, he had hired young hooligans to antagonise people around Jeremy Jones' demonstrations, in order to discredit the Labour movement and to provoke a vigorous reaction in the pro-Brexit camp. Since the end of June, the police had been tracking down the perpetrators, using CCTV from the surrounding streets. After long enquiries they had managed to arrest several of them. At first, they had all said they had acted alone. But in more recent weeks some had begun to talk, revealing the existence of a network traced back to Guy Wick.

Tracy placed the note on her desk. This was huge. If it was true, public opinion would not forgive Wick's actions. The British people had been deeply shocked by the outbreaks of violence since the end of June. Jeremy Jones had been blamed, even though he had denied any involvement and blamed rogue elements. Anyway, no facts incriminating him had come to light. If now it was proved that the events were part of a Machiavellian scheme by his main opponent, a wave of public anger would hit Wick like a tsunami.

The Prime Minister was thinking fast. Guy Wick, an extremely intelligent politician, was known for his lack of scruples. His political cunning was legendary, as was his ability to set traps for his enemies to fall into. But from that to using violence ... Tracy could not believe it without having irrefutable evidence. She knew, however, that not everyone would be as cautious as her. The news was going to come out in the papers. The result would be a media storm. But behind Guy Wick, there was also the Conservative party and the conference the following Saturday. Whether or not Guy Wick had acted improperly, it was necessary at all costs to preserve the reputation of the party, which had certainly not been involved in these schemes.

Still at her desk, Tracy telephoned the Home Secretary. He told her that the investigation was continuing, looking for evidence other than the witness statements. He expressed his fears that the press would soon get hold of the case, despite the precautions taken by the police.

The next day in fact the news was all over the papers. They even gave more information, including the exact statement of one of the middlemen who had given the young thugs their orders. He said he had received money from one of Guy Wick's representatives to pay them. During the morning, the Conservative politician was asked to report to a police station for questioning. He obeyed the summons immediately. When he left, three hours later, he made a statement in front of cameras from all the national TV stations, protesting his complete innocence, reminding them that he had devoted his life to politics for the public good, not to organise violence. He claimed it was all a plot cooked up by his political opponents.

On Tuesday morning, one of the broadsheets published extracts of emails from him, sent to someone calling himself Mr Task, encouraging attacks and specifying the methods to use. Wick made more statements on the radio, denying it all, stating that the emails were faked. But he had lost all public credibility and the media frenzy intensified in the afternoon when the police revealed that they had recordings of telephone conversations, which were currently being analysed. On Wednesday, the CPS announced they would be bringing a criminal case, on the basis of the evidence so far received.

In the court of the media and social networks, Guy Wick had already been tried and convicted. Newspaper editorials were full of attacks on a man "who had dishonoured British politics and the pro-Brexit movement". On the same day in Parliament, Jeremy Jones cautiously declared that he could not imagine Guy Wick resorting to such methods and put his faith in the judicial process. Some Labour MPs, however, began to ask whether in fact the Conservative party had been behind Wick's actions. Tracy reacted vigorously, denying that the party had any involvement – which there was not a shadow of evidence to suggest – and hoping that the legal system would carry out its investigations as swiftly as possible. Several Conservative MPs attacked Labour for seeking to make political capital from the case. The Speaker had to suspend the sitting as insults flew from both sides of the House. The political climate was becoming poisonous. One thing was clear though: the majority of Conservative MPs wanted a line drawn between Guy Wick and the party as quickly as possible. That afternoon there was a clamour of calls for his immediate resignation.

Guy Wick understood that he was helpless in the face of the tide of public opinion. He decided he would have to accept the situation. That same evening, he made a statement on television in which he reaffirmed his innocence and announced, with a heavy heart, his resignation from the Conservative Party and his withdrawal from political life until his name was cleared. He said that he would devote his time entirely to defending himself. In just three days, the most popular politician in Britain after Jeremy Jones, the man who was about to bring down the Prime Minister, had himself been brought down, brutally and completely out of the blue.

His disappearance left a vacuum in the Brexit political landscape. Wick had been the undisputed leader of the movement for years, and personally involved at the forefront for months of the campaign, so he was obviously difficult to replace, with no official deputy. But above all, there was an immediate decamping of the MPs who had been of his persuasion. They saw the party falling apart and many realised that their electoral prospects were not good. It was also becoming difficult to support a movement which was accused, even indirectly, of serious malpractice. On the day of the party conference, a third of the MPs who had previously supported Guy Wick announced that there were good points to the new European structure and that it might not be incompatible with national sovereignty. They joined the Prime Minister's camp. Another third of the deputies did not attend the conference, announcing the day before that they were leaving the party to join UKIP which was beginning to see a political renaissance. The remaining third remained stalwart, voting for a candidate rounded up at the last minute, who had nothing of the charisma of Guy Wick. By the end of the vote, late in the afternoon, Tracy, who everyone had given up for lost a week earlier, was confirmed in her position as party leader, winning the vote by a large majority.

The new Europe

The Prime Minister devoted the last weeks of 2022 to discussions on the outlines of the proposed new treaty with her European colleagues. The concept of a "flexible Union", supported by many heads of state, had made significant progress between September and November. Most governments saw it as an opportunity to renegotiate provisions that were not favourable to their countries under current European arrangements. According to the most enthusiastic supporters of the reform, the new treaty would make the Union a dynamic area of political, economic and cultural cooperation, with varying levels of participation, each country choosing the programmes it wished to participate in and retaining full sovereignty over the legislative provisions that concerned it. In France, the leaders of the Democratic Alliance, who claimed to have been the authors of the reform, spoke of it in terms of a real revolution relaunching the European ideal for the benefit of the people.

The reality of the proposed changes was much more subtle. The treaty was being drafted by a large committee, representing all the countries and various interest groups. They shared one objective: to make the Union more democratic, to bring it closer to the people, to renew the spirit of the European project. But once these basic principles had been laid down, the debates became intense between the proponents of a decentralised union, a Europe of nations, and those who wanted to maintain a powerful decision-making centre in Brussels, organising convergence to transcend the selfish interests of each state. The former argued that the increases in the Union's powers with each successive treaty had resulted in a technocratic superstructure, disconnected from the electorate, and so now they would have to put the machine into reverse. Their opponents, on the contrary, claimed that each increase in remit had been designed to solve the problems caused by an incomplete union, and that you should not write off sixty-five years of institutional experience. Beyond their differences of opinion, the members of the committee were well aware of how high the stakes were in this drafting work: if agreement could not be reached, the very structure of Europe could collapse under the weight of popular discontent. Over the last few years several countries, led by nationalist or just protectionist governments, had threatened to throw off the shackles of the community regulations or even to leave the Union if they were not given satisfaction on essential points regarding sovereignty.

The discussions resulted in a compromise, which differed from the initial plan drawn up by the Democratic Alliance. When the completed first draft of the treaty was presented for review by the member states, in mid-November, the main philosophical principles of the Union – democracy, respect for the individual, solidarity between nations – were reaffirmed and strengthened, and any deviation from them could result in the country concerned being expelled from the Union in cases of serious misconduct. The single market and the customs union remained the essential economic foundations of the Union. Beyond this non-negotiable core, the remaining areas, unlike in previous treaties, were open to nations to participate in on an à la carte or selective basis. This covered currency management (the Euro), foreign policy, defence, space, taxation, justice, education, health, agriculture, energy, and the environment, all except for the minimum rules ensuring coherence and the efficient functioning of the common market.

The reaffirmation of the single market entailed the continuing need for a strong European Commission. Its primary role was still the development of unified commercial standards, common consumer and environment protection provisions and criteria for fair economic competition. It ensured that the employment law and social security structures of the various member countries reflected the humanistic ambitions of the Union while avoiding obvious distortions. In addition to this standardising work, it had to promote European industrial and economic projects and co-ordinate the process of selective cooperation. It would lead the negotiation of international trade agreements, including the imposition of special taxes on goods and services from countries that were not sufficiently aligned with European Community social law. Over its entire scope of action, it was subject to an obligation to regularly assess the performance of the policies followed, as well as to monitor compliance with international agreements signed by the Union, and propose amendments if necessary. It was to be judged by its results, using criteria based on the continent's economic and social progress.

Several community rules were reviewed. The four fundamental freedoms were upheld – free movement of people, goods, capital and services – but these freedoms could be modified by member countries, in a more sustainable and stronger way than before, to protect certain strategic interests or avoid major imbalances, provided the country could justify the restrictions. The quorum for decision making at the Council on which each government was represented would become stricter, to ensure that only decisions with a large majority could be passed on matters involving the single market and trade agreements: the basic majority was raised to 75% of the countries, representing at least 75% of the population, instead of 55% and 65% respectively. This change, the result of intense negotiations, was designed to promote proposals that attracted broad consensus. It had the result of rendering unworkable any decision opposed by France and Germany simultaneously (or the United Kingdom if it rejoined the Union), given the size of the population of these countries. In the areas open to selective participation, the Council's vote was not subject to majority rules, as it was designed only to identify countries wishing to participate in specific initiatives.

The procedure for parliamentary adoption of European laws was radically changed: instead of first going before the European Parliament, the regulations and directives prepared by the European Commission would be approved by the Council and, if ratified, would then be sent to the national parliaments. They had six months to approve the texts, either in the prescribed form, in the case of mandatory regulations, or with local adaptations, for directives. In the event of 25% of the parliaments rejecting the proposals, there would be a second draft submission, once the commission had revised the texts, taking into account the objections that had been submitted. If the second draft was rejected, the text would be considered as unadopted, with the countries who were in favour remaining free to apply it, on the principle of voluntary participation, or to withdraw it. This procedure significantly strengthened the European Union's national base, as members of national parliaments were close to their constituents and directly answerable to them. The Commission, while preparing the legal texts, was obliged to work both with the governments, who ratified the legislation via the Council, and with the national parliaments, to ensure their support. The European Parliament itself would not be dissolved, as the Democratic Alliance had requested, but, having lost its legislative function, was assigned a role more of strategic orientation for the Union, debating European projects and representing public opinion. It managed the Commission and approved the European budget. The Court of Justice of the European Union would remain a central body but its scope of action was limited to the essential areas of the Union.

There was a great deal of media debate over the draft treaty. Opponents were critical of the à la carte participation model, which they believed would create a "patchwork" Europe or encourage instinctive protectionism. They warned of the risk of a complex and obscure Europe if uniformity of laws was to be abolished. They asked how the European budget would be distributed, as each country would be contributing to different programmes. They were highly critical of the process for enacting legislation through national parliaments, which would complicate the development of common texts and paralyse decisions. They warned that the new organisation would prevent Europe from building any kind of federal system similar to the United States in future. The President of the European Parliament protested against the removal of legislative powers from his institution. But all that had little effect on public opinion: the popular mood was in favour of a democratic loosening of regulation and on the whole the draft treaty was welcomed. Generally, people believed that you could not force twenty-seven countries to operate according to the same rules and that a new-found flexibility would, on the contrary, enable Europe to operate more dynamically. And the President of the European Parliament himself eventually recognised the benefits of focussing parliamentary work on debating strategic issues, with the opportunity for citizens' views on them to be represented.

The real innovation that was particularly popular, apart from the institutional reforms, was the second part of the work of the advisory committee: the European Commission should, within a period of twelve months, identify all the issues of contention from the national governments regarding how the Union operated, as well as their proposals for projects to be carried out at European level. Citizens would also be consulted and invited to submit their proposals on the Internet. On the basis of this analysis, the Commission would then draw up an action plan to be debated in the Council. The primary goal was to solve the practical difficulties faced by countries, such as joint management of borders, competition which would be classed as unfair between countries with different standards of living, or problems with trade agreements with third countries. In addition, on the basis of surveys that would be carried out, the Commission would have to propose major initiatives allowing co-operation on the new selective basis, for example on new technologies, solidarity, education, or the environment. Several popular topics had emerged outside the areas of economic issues: the creation of a European humanitarian intervention force, which would represent the Union in the event of a disaster in an overseas country; a major educational project based on enhancing the Erasmus programme; an initiative for the disabled and equal opportunities. The treaty established a formal process of drawing up European strategic plans, to be regularly revised, taking into account the aspirations of citizens, governments and European institutions, with a clear bias towards achieving concrete projects. It was a break with the idea, true or not, of a Europe built solely on the initiatives of the Brussels authorities. The process clearly established the responsibilities of all parties.

European leaders agreed that they would approve the text at a special summit in December and that 2023 would be devoted to its ratification by member countries with a proposed date for entry into force of 1st January 2024.

* * *

Tracy immediately realised the advantages of the draft treaty, which would allow her country to re-enter the European market while maintaining control over key aspects.

Thanks to her personal relationships with her fellow government leaders, and also via John Klin, who was able to appear as an expert before the committee, she managed to make the UK's voice heard on some important provisions, even though her country was not directly represented in the drafting committee of the treaty. For example, she managed to have the possibility of imposing quotas on intra-European immigration included. Most importantly, she received confirmation from the Council that a UK reapplication for membership would be accepted and welcome. On November 30th, 2022, in a landmark speech in Parliament, she sketched the outlines of a possible return to the European Union starting in 2024, if the treaty went ahead with the clauses she was hoping for. She was at pains to word her statement very carefully, emphasising the many conditions that would have to be fulfilled before such membership could be formally envisaged. She specified that the government would only make a specific proposal in January, once the final text of the European treaty was known, and only if the essential conditions on sovereignty were met. She added that the proposal would be put to a vote both in Parliament and to the whole country, with further details to be confirmed at a later date. The session was stormy. The MPs still loyal to Guy Wick, who was under investigation and so not present, were very vocal in their disagreement, to the point that proceedings had to be suspended. Tracy was well aware of the risk of a Conservative

Party split. She had thought long and hard and taken advice before making her announcement. But she had judged that, unlike last February, the situation was now such that she had a chance of success. The financial markets equally welcomed her statement with a new sharp rise; however, they would ultimately remain cautious until the government proposal in January.

The afternoon following the parliamentary session, Tracy received a message from James Callagher. He congratulated her on her statement, which, according to him, was going in the right direction. He assured her of his support and informed her that his club would contact a number of MPs to get them on side for the idea of a return to Europe. He did not expect a reply, which made it easier for Tracy, who did not want to be implicated in the billionaire's schemes.

The May 2023 campaign

At the beginning of January 2023, the government concluded its study on the new Europe. The European treaty had been signed by the Heads of State, including the terms the UK had hoped for, and had taken the UK's points into account. On the same day, Tracy announced that she would lead the Conservative Party in the May General Election on a platform of Britain's membership application for the new Union. No action would be taken before the General Election, but if her party achieved a majority, the government would embark on the accession process after a Parliamentary vote. Half the Conservative MPs were in favour of the Prime Minister's plan. The Labour Party, represented by Jeremy Jones, supported the proposal but did not fail to point out the Conservatives' U-turn. Several Conservative MPs resigned from the party and joined UKIP. The newspapers relished the irony of seeing a Prime Minister who had campaigned in 2018 on the basis of Brexit XXL announce that she would now be campaigning on a diametrically opposite platform.

The financial markets leapt 6% on the day Tracy confirmed she was standing. Whilst there was still some electoral uncertainty, UKIP's chances of taking Labour or Conservative votes were thought to be relatively low. The markets were already betting on Britain's return to the European common market in 2024. The pound rose sharply in the days that followed, as Callagher had predicted.

Tracy had a clear vision of the election campaign she was planning to run. To combat UKIP she needed to show that the new European order was the right choice for the country. She knew that it would be difficult to convince all the people who had supported Brexit, but she hoped to attract at least a part of this electorate who, in the absence of Guy Wick, would be prepared to listen to the objective arguments in favour of the new Union. She would also have to take on Jeremy Jones, the only major opponent, in the area of domestic politics. She had always appealed to low earners, people who were struggling. She would be touring the regions that were suffering economically, and she would emphasise all the initiatives she had taken, and that she was planning to strengthen, to restore the purchasing power of low income groups.

★ ★ ★

On January 14th, however, there was another political bolt from the blue. The CPS enquiry declared Guy Wick totally innocent of the charges against him. The incitement to violence over the summer of 2022 was not down to him: the witness statements were falsehoods, the e-mails that had been seized, as well as the recordings of his voice, had been faked with elaborate computer trickery. It was also established that Guy Wick could not have physically sent some of the messages, because he had concrete alibis. The mystery of who had in fact arranged for the attacks still remained, but Guy Wick was cleared of all suspicion. That evening a large crowd of well-wishers gathered at the senior

Conservative's house to show their support. The next day, Wick announced his return to politics, not in the Conservative Party but as the leader of a new structure, the Party for Great Britain, which was to be a merger of his Tory defectors and UKIP. The party's campaign platform would very openly centre on rejection of any application to rejoin the European Union. In a few days, half of the remaining Conservative MPs joined the movement, definitively confirming a party split, with the party fracturing along the lines of divide on the European issue. Given Guy Wick's restored popularity, the Party for Great Britain shot ahead in the polls: in early February, they were at 35%, against 25% for the Conservatives. Jeremy Jones' Labour Party, driven by the younger generation and a desire amongst many voters for a complete change in government, was predicted at 40%. The outcome of the General Election in May was far from predetermined, although analysts were keen to highlight the most important point, namely that 65% of people supported parties that were behind the new EU project.

Jeremy Jones proved to be a very good campaign strategist. Since September, while the Conservative party was tearing itself apart, he had travelled the length and breadth of the country and brought his points home. His strategies were beginning to pay off: people appreciated his consistency, his enthusiasm, his charisma as much as the innovative nature of his proposals. Most importantly, he had understood that some of the electorate were still concerned about how expensive his programme would be, because of the scale of the social projects and the investments he was proposing. From February, while ensuring he retained his most iconic proposals, he significantly reduced his spending plans and produced more realistic revenue forecasts. He was positioning himself as a serious leader the country could put its trust in.

Tracy, on the other hand, was soon confronted with the contradictions inherent in her policy. She faced the same problem as during the run-up to the Conservative Party conference: having campaigned on Brexit XXL in 2018, it was very difficult for her to explain why she was now fighting for a return to the European Union; however much she argued that it was not the same Union any more, the journalists had her on the back foot, and often managed to trip her up. Nor could she claim to have had great success with her economic policy, given the dire situation that had prevailed under her government. The situation had been improving steadily since October, though. The financial markets and the pound were gradually rising, confidence was returning, and investments were picking up; 2023 could be the first year since 2019 to show positive growth. But that was not going to be nearly enough for voters, who held Tracy primarily responsible for the difficulties that the country was going through.

In an attempt to protect the Prime Minister from the criticisms levelled at her by the Party for Great Britain, her supporters argued that her historic support for Brexit was clear proof of her commitment to British sovereignty. The change of policy was based on a pragmatic analysis of what the country had gone through, as well as the opportunities created by the new European structure. Guy Wick was accused of blindness and stubbornness where everything pointed to the need for a new direction. But an election campaign is not the best place for complex arguments. The electorate could not get past a straightforward equation: Meller had led the Brexit XXL policy, she had failed, she had to go. The lead-up to the election was a long slow martyrdom for the Conservative Party, which fell little by little, week by week in the polls, losing voters mainly to the Labour Party. Some MPs argued for a change of leader, most suggesting that the Chancellor of the Exchequer should stand. But it was too late for that kind of strategy. In any event, no one was jostling for the position at the head of the troops in those conditions and the Chancellor himself reaffirmed his loyalty to Tracy.

Guy Wick, for his part, had the advantage of consistency. He expanded on his usual argument that the difficulties that Great Britain had experienced were not due, intrinsically, to Brexit, but to Tracy Meller's inability to negotiate trade agreements, the inadequacy of government industrial policy, and repeated fraud by speculators controlled by international financial institutions. If strong trade agreements had been signed, the country, instead of being weakened, could have genuinely benefited from its new freedom to develop its foreign trade. Guy Wick put himself forward to lead a government that would finally put this policy in place. However, despite an active campaign, he was unable to gain a voter base higher than the 35% his supporters represented, because after six difficult years, Brexit had lost its appeal for most people outside the core of die-hard Leavers. Worsening bit by bit, Wick's support gradually dwindled, as his followers sensed the inevitable approach of defeat.

On Thursday, May 4th, 2023, in a historic General Election, the Labour Party won 52% of the vote and an absolute majority in Parliament. The Party for Great Britain polled 29%, and the Conservative Party was defeated with 13%, an absolute rout. A handful of minor parties shared the remaining 6%. Tracy made a very noble speech declaring her government at an end. The next day, Jeremy Jones, once an unemployed carpenter, now leader of a Labour Party he had thoroughly reformed, became Prime Minister of the United Kingdom, appointed by the Queen. In his first speech as Prime Minister, he promised the British people a referendum on the European Union in June 2024. The City welcomed the election results with a further rise in the financial markets. The Scottish Parliament announced the suspension of its request for another independence referendum. James Callagher sent his congratulations to the new Prime Minister.

A last weekend in Chequers

Tracy spent the weekend of May 6th and 7th at Chequers. Jeremy Jones had kindly permitted her one last stay at the residence. The former Prime Minister, accompanied by her husband, reluctantly abandoned this beautiful house where she had spent the happiest days of her term of office. Beyond the bitterness of defeat, she felt, paradoxically, a feeling of relief. The mission she had set for herself had been too onerous. She had seen in the challenge of Brexit the opportunity for the personal commitment she sought, and she had wanted to lead the country to freer and happier days and had believed herself capable of doing so. But she had experienced a constant succession of ordeals, trapped by her desire to serve her country. A more cynical politician, less determined in his moral principles, would have either tried to avoid the position, leaving others to face the problems, or changed policy sooner, betraying his empty promises, finding a political rationale for it. But not her: she had received a mandate from the voters and she had been determined to stick to it. It was only when she was really at the end of her tether, after the major crisis of 2022 and its consequences, that she had allowed herself to consider another direction, luckily just as Europe itself was changing. Despite everything, she was proud of what she had accomplished: she had loyally implemented what the country had asked for, without resorting to any deceit. Admittedly, the experience had proved bitter. But the very fact that these times had been so testing would ensure that Britain's choice to join Europe again was a long lasting one. Whatever Guy Wick said, it would have been difficult to implement Brexit XXL in any other way. And a more flexible Brexit, even assuming that it would have been politically possible given the circumstances, which she doubted, would not have been any easier or more beneficial for the country: its long-term consequences, less visible, might well have been more insidious. In the end, the hard Brexit experience had been necessary, and it had fallen to her, Tracy Meller, to orchestrate it. She had only one real regret: that she had not been able to unite the country. As it was, more than 65% of voters had voted for parties in favour of the new European Union. But nearly 30% had supported Wick, and many Brexit supporters had abstained. Of course it would be idealistic to think that there would be anything like unanimity on this subject, but she would have liked to see a more definitive result. Since there was a year left before the referendum, she vowed to support Jeremy Jones, who now had the job of healing the divides in the country. Although Jones was from a different party, she wanted him to succeed now, for the good of the country.

★ ★ ★

On Saturday afternoon, Tracy allowed herself one final walk. Leaving the grounds, she climbed nearby Coombe Hill, which had a beautiful view. She breathed the pure air amongst the trees, took a good long walk and ran into a lot of other walkers. Having been nervous about meeting people after the bitter defeat that the country had just inflicted on her, she was touched by the kindness of her fellow citizens. Many thanked her for the integrity with which she had served her country and praised her dignified handover speech, leaving her feeling very moved. Further on, when she had reached the summit, she looked out over the magnificent view of the surrounding valley. She was alone, with tears in her eyes, thinking of the strange way things had turned out, when suddenly she saw a red kite take off from a nearby tree. The wide brown and red wings unfolded in smooth flight, carrying the bird of prey high into the blue sky. She watched it for a long time, wondering if it was going to go north, or to bank south, over Chequers. It chose north. She slowly retraced her steps, on the path home. On the way down she spotted the brown house in the middle of the trees below her, and she thought back to Sir Arthur Lee's declaration. Had Chequers helped her in her life as Prime Minister? Her most important decisions had undoubtedly been taken in London: calling the election in 2018, the unilateral exit from the European Union, the continuation of her policy in February 2022 in spite of the crisis that was brewing, her U-turn in September 2022: it was in the capital that she had taken all these resolutions, after consulting with her Ministers, her experts, the Governor of the Bank of England, her colleagues or opposition MPs, and of course the Queen. At each of these key moments, she had been alone, like all Prime Ministers, in making the final choices, after having received all the various opinions, and alone in shouldering the responsibility. Yet she also felt that the peaceful surroundings of Chequers had been intimately linked to her decisions. There had been visits, like those of Laura Soriens and John Klin, not so long ago, as well as those of Jeremy Jones and Guy Wick, which she remembered with amusement. Chequers had allowed for informal discussions, in a setting quite different to that of the capital. There had also been the long walks, and evenings alone with her husband. There had been, quite simply, the fresh air and relaxation of the countryside. In fact, the more she thought about it, Tracy realised it was not between 2016 and 2018 that Chequers had really influenced her. Her decisions at the time were driven by one simple goal: to implement Brexit. It was when the serious difficulties had begun, when the first doubts had appeared, from the end of 2019, that she had felt the need to use the residence for something other than relaxing on weekends. It was then that she had begun to invite guests whose opinions differed from hers, as she had also done at the Savoy. That was how she had gradually become imbued with the tranquillity of this peaceful place, especially during her long walks. After years of ideological government, she had gradually accepted that there is no one absolute truth, that there is always another way of viewing reality. She had admitted to doubts, at least in private. Going down this path during 2020-2021 had allowed her, at last, to really ask herself the difficult questions the following year. But the period of office of a Prime Minister is only a wing beat in the long slow flight of a nation. Hers had finished. After coming down the hill she went to the house to spend her last few hours there. Her bags were packed and tomorrow she would leave Chequers. But she knew now she would come back to this part of the world.

Referendum

On June 20th, 2024, Jeremy Jones invited Tracy, in a private capacity, to Downing Street, to watch the results of the referendum with him. The first exit polls suggested that the Yes vote would carry it with more than 70% of votes, on a very high turnout. The Prime Minister came out in front of Number 10 and gave a speech. The main thrust of it was widely quoted:

"The British people have decided to turn a new page in their history by joining, as a full member, the reformed European Union, thus ending the Brexit experiment voted in eight years ago. This is not just a decision based on logic, it is one that comes from the heart. Logic dictates that our country, with all the industrial, financial, and commercial sectors of its economy, will benefit greatly from its return to the most active market in the world. Our workers will benefit from social rights developed by a community with a long tradition of protecting workers' rights. Our economic progress will be boosted. Our businesses will be stimulated by more open competition. Our nation, which has always promoted economic freedom, will regain its natural place in this group, without compromising the essential components of its sovereignty. However, this decision, as I said, also comes from the heart. Our nation's history, which we can feel very proud of, is global, but its roots are, and have always been, European. Our fellow citizens could not stand back from being part of writing the pages of the future history of Europe. We belong to this beautiful community with whom, beneath superficial national differences, we share fundamental values. It was inconceivable that we should remain on the outside. We can rightly aspire to a common future with our neighbours, and wholeheartedly dream of a European ideal, to which we will contribute.

"The period of Brexit has been violent and difficult. I was always critical of it. But History will show it was not in vain. Without it, the European Union would probably not have had the courage to question itself so deeply. Without it, our country might not go forward with the same resolution as we do today, having experienced the price of isolation.

"What Europe will become is not written down anywhere. It is up to us, the citizens, to invent it, and I am proud to know that the British people will once again be full participants in this future."

Epilogue

Or: What they did after the referendum.

Jane Farrow, the Governor of the Bank of England's mother-in-law, was tidying her kitchen. She threw away the bottle of cheap spirits she had been using since 2021 to prepare and set light to her Christmas puddings. She took her good bottle out from the bottom of a cupboard. "This can come out of hiding now, I think, he's understood the point," she said to herself as she dusted the glass off. A small silent laugh flitted across her face when she thought about her nephew, who she had sent out to throw pudding at Philip Denniel. "We had to show him that it could not go on." The end justifies the means...

Philip Denniel, unaware of his mother-in-law's machinations, was walking his Labrador in the fine weather on June 21st. He was hoping he was done with financial crises for good and was looking forward to some peaceful times at the head of the

Bank of England. Would he ever be accused of being paid to do nothing again?

Tracy Meller, having returned from London, did a spot of gardening before going for a lovely country walk. With the royalties from the sale of her memoirs she had bought a cottage in the Chilterns, where she and her husband were enjoying a peaceful retirement.

Janet Gradens went to work in the public library in a small suburban town. She had been discharged from the psychiatric hospital a year earlier. Her doctors were very pleased with her rehabilitation. Patrick had not come back to her, but she had started dating someone she liked a lot.

John Klin was cursing himself. He had decided to defrag the hard drive of his computer and had just deleted his most recent article by mistake. It had shown, with data to prove it, that the crisis of February 2022 was the work of speculators, who had been planning their attacks since the year before. Klin did have a backup of the document, but he couldn't remember where he had put it. He had intended to make it the last chapter of his book on the economic history of Brexit, which he was due to publish the following month. "Too bad," he said to himself, and went out for a walk, deciding to publish his book as it was and to give up research on the Brexit period to work on forecasting the new economic future of the country.

Luke Trosden met James Callagher at his house in Kensington Palace Gardens. Over a fine whisky, they reminisced about their years of stock market speculation. Their best deals had been done during the crisis of 2022. With the support of several members of the Financial Club, they had triggered the stock market panic

EPILOGUE

in February and had kept the markets low for several months. They had then bought when prices were at their lowest, and were now reaping huge profits, taking advantage of the new markets made possible by the referendum. The real stroke of genius, for which they toasted each other in self-satisfied congratulation, was the temporary fall of Guy Wick, which they had cleverly, and discreetly, organised at just the right moment, setting in motion the chain of events which had led to the end of Brexit – the ultimate aim of Callagher's "master plan". No one knew that Luke had arranged the attacks over the summer to set Wick up. In the end, during the elections, the Club had not supported Tracy Meller's Conservatives, abandoning them to an inevitable defeat, and accepting that Jones would win, so long as he guaranteed a return to Europe and a more reasonable economic programme. The Club, however, strongly supported the "Yes" campaign in the June 2024 referendum.

Laura Soriens met with her board of directors: the HGB bank had got back to a stable financial situation and could consider refunding the capital the State had injected into it as part of its bail-out two years earlier.

Nick Walderg took Friday off and spent a long weekend at the seaside with Nancy. He and his friend Mark Tweeds had founded an Internet start-up that was going very well.

Jeremy Jones had talks with several leaders of member states of the Union, including the German Chancellor and President Marquet, who congratulated him, and they exchanged ideas for major European projects.

Guy Wick was in a bad mood all day. But that did not stop him from carrying on the work he had been doing every day for a year. He was making careful note of all Jeremy Jones' mistakes. He had been up and down the country gathering problems and grumbles. Now he was going to meticulously catalogue the disadvantages of the new Europe. Yes, the country had voted. But the election campaign of 2028 would come round, and with it the opportunity to make the voters reconsider their strategic choices. And, perhaps one day, to find and punish those who had brought him down at the very moment when he was about to become Prime Minister.

THE END

Addendum: Brexit from 2016 to 2021

(Extract from: **Economic History of Brexit**, published by John Klin, July 25th, 2024, Introduction to Chapter 1: "Brexit from 2016 to 2021")

When the British people voted to leave the European Union in June 2016, the initial situation looked promising. Admittedly, the value of the pound fell sharply in the aftermath of the referendum, a sign that the markets were unnerved, but the government then made much of the country's newfound competitiveness. Tax incentives were put in place to attract foreign investors. The economy went well for the first few months, which was far from being the catastrophe promised by many economists before the vote. Prime Minister Meller, who was appointed in July 2016 following the resignation of her predecessor, repeatedly stated that Brexit would be an opportunity for Britain. Her aim was straightforward: to implement the voters' decision to leave the European Union, while negotiating a privileged trade agreement guaranteeing continued access to the Continental market, the only point that really mattered for the British economy.

Mrs Meller spent the first months of her term defining the outlines of her idea of Brexit. She dismissed a so-called "Norwegian-style" solution. This solution consisted in leaving the European Union while remaining a member of the European Economic Area, subject to the payment of an annual contribution to the Union's budget and the acceptance of the four fundamental freedoms: movement of persons, goods, capital and services. This solution would allow the country to benefit from the economic advantages of the Union while avoiding its political constraints. The payment of a contribution was, however, a very delicate subject, as the Brexit Leave campaign had put a great deal of emphasis on wanting British money to stay in Britain instead of going to Brussels. There was also a major political problem: freedom of movement of people, a necessary condition for a Norwegian-style agreement, did not address the desire of many voters to limit intra-European immigration. Mrs Meller chose not to be hampered by the conditions of that possible solution. She opted for a complete exit from the European Union and the European Economic Area, accompanied by a straightforward trade agreement. After several months preparing her strategy, she was convinced that she was going into the negotiations with a winning hand. She persuaded herself that Europe would make all the required concessions, because the countries still in the Union with profitable trading relationships with the United Kingdom could not risk a trade agreement failing.

Mrs Meller thus invoked the famous Article 50 of the Treaty on European Union in March 2017, which gave the country two years to organise the terms of departure and to define future economic relations.

Unfortunately, nothing after that went according to her plans.

Mrs Meller started the negotiations with a great many requirements, which was a tactical mistake. These British demands, which might have been acceptable in less eventful times, worried European negotiators anxious to show the public that an exit from the European Union was accompanied by significant loss of benefits, in order to discourage any other country from following the UK's example. In addition, 2017 was an election year in both France and Germany. There was no mileage for their leaders in being accommodating towards the UK. Berlin gave a definitive response to Mrs Meller's demands: "No to 'à la carte' negotiations".

The European Commission adopted a firm approach to the discussions: before any negotiations on future trade relations, the very issue Mrs Meller wished to address first, they would have to reach agreement on the key principles of leaving the Union. This agreement should include the contribution to be paid by Great Britain to settle its accounts, based on all of its existing commitments, as well as sensitive subjects such as the protection of the rights of European citizens after Brexit and the issue of the land border with Northern Ireland.

These complex discussions dragged on until the end of the year, finally coming to an end in December with a hard-won agreement at the price of many concessions and against the backdrop of internal political divisions within the government and Mrs Meller's Conservative party.

There was only a year left to negotiate a trade agreement, when these types of discussions normally take several years. Key economic players began to be nervous. Investments collapsed. Immigration fell, leading to a shortage of manpower. Many banks in London began the planned transfer of their activities to Frankfurt, Amsterdam, Dublin, Paris, or Luxembourg, who had all rolled out the red carpet for them.

Mrs Meller came under strong political pressure but thought she would be able to conclude negotiations before the deadline. However, the trade negotiations started to go badly, rapidly becoming mired in endless deliberations. In response to British demands, each country responded with specific requirements, such as one country wanting to defend its farmers, another one its manufacturing industry, and so on. The Brussels negotiators, subject to pressure from their respective countries, were no longer able to keep to a unified strategy which could lead to agreement. The situation reached crisis point in March 2018, when the European Commission, under pressure from President Marquet's representatives, refused point blank to accept British requests for access to the European market for their banks and their services industry, stating that this access could only be granted by paying a very high annual contribution. This position was unacceptable to the British. It caused a torrent of anti-European rants in the British media. Under pressure from public opinion and her party, Mrs Meller decided that the negotiations were a dead end. She took a completely new political direction: since we had to have Brexit, then Brexit it would be, completely, immediately, and with no negotiations. An all-out Brexit. No holds barred. XXL size. While on one hand this would entail a difficult economic transition with Europe, Britain would regain complete freedom to make deals with other countries in the world. Perhaps even the Europeans, whose trade with the United Kingdom would be directly affected, would be obliged to make compromises.

To gain a mandate for her policy, Meller called a General Election for May 2018, which she believed she could win comfortably, surfing on a wave of riled British public opinion. Since the 2011 Fixed-Term Parliament Act, the Prime Minister was no longer free to call early elections. The right to do so was in the give of Parliament, by a two-thirds vote or a vote of no confidence. With the Conservative Party's agreement to dissolve Parliament, Mrs Meller was able to gain the support of the Labour Party, whose leader had misjudged the electoral situation, thinking that an election in these difficult circumstances would be to Labour's advantage. Parliament therefore approved an election. A short campaign began at once. Mrs Meller promised an end to compromises, a return to total freedom for the country after its break with the European authorities, and one simple slogan: "100% British". These promises went down well with the public, who had been irritated by the constant stream of European requirements since 2017. The Labour Party could not stop the momentum: Mrs Meller's Conservative Party won by a landslide in May 2018. As a result of these elections, Parliament voted to break off all negotiations. Britain would leave the Union in March 2019, at the end of the two years provided for in Article 50, without any agreement other than some transitional arrangements.

The government knew full well that the country would start to see effects straight away from tariffs and legal complexities which would now affect trade with Europe. They were counting on it strengthening national industries. As tariffs would be high, it would be cheaper to make products in Britain. Domestic production would be radically stimulated, which would create jobs and drive consumption. In addition, because of the pound's fall in value, British exports would become competitive in the international market and there would be growth in export business. The new economic agreements negotiated with various countries would reinforce this trend, triggering a virtuous cycle of economic growth. This argument had been at the heart of the election campaign, selling the voters on the bright future under Brexit XXL.

Unfortunately, domestic industries were not prepared for this shock treatment, having dwindled considerably or relocated production internationally in recent decades as a result of the globalised economy. Such industry as remained had to import the raw materials required for production anyway, which had now become expensive. Now suffering penalties on trade with Europe, they no longer had the benefit of a market dynamic enough to provide good return on their investment. In addition, they began to struggle to obtain bank financing as British banks were themselves affected by Brexit.

In addition, even with a devalued pound, domestic production remained expensive compared to Asian countries, especially China, which dominated the markets. In Europe, Germany, anxious to preserve its economic power, pushed the European Union to take protectionist measures to protect itself from cheap British imports. Ireland, whose corporation tax rate was traditionally low, benefited fully from its new status as the only English-speaking member of the Union, attracting many international investors who would otherwise have gone to Britain. Spain, Portugal and Eastern Europe, who offered competitive production costs, gained market share. In short, the Brexit result swiftly turned to disaster for British industry, which had to refocus on domestic production as best it could. The blow was cushioned by a strong national rally: encouraged by the Prime Minister, the British concentrated on purchasing products "Made in Britain". This remarkable civic effort allowed industry to survive to a certain extent but could not prevent underlying trends and numerous corporate insolvencies.

The government looked for opportunities within the Commonwealth, with whom the UK had a special relationship. However, Britain's trade with these countries was in deficit overall and the fall in value of the pound only worsened this situation.

Mrs Meller was also disappointed on the other side of the Atlantic. The 45th US President, Mr T., elected late in 2016 after a very aggressive campaign, had initially promised all his support. He had been one of the few statesmen to be encouraging about Brexit. "Get out of there," he had said to Britain. "Set your country free to thrive. Drop the old Europe." He had promised a swift trade deal. Five years on this promise had still not been kept. The delay had not just been a result of the complexity of commercial negotiations with the US administration. The United States had quickly taken a dim view of Britain's steadfast commitment to developing digital industries, which competed directly with their computer giants. The Americans were also wary of the British willingness to promote research, especially medical research, seeing it as potentially dangerous competition. All of these were factors in the stalling of negotiations on a trade deal.

Discussions with China were no more fruitful. This venerable country, in its wisdom, politely replied that it would take time to see how Britain's economy would work in a post-Brexit environment, before they could start discussions on a specific agreement. In the meantime, trade could be carried out under World Trade Organisation rules. Moreover, the Chinese representatives, familiar with the thousands of years of history of their country, and aware of the price of unity as well as that of disunity, expressed doubts about the relevance and durability of Brexit XXL.

The economic situation in Great Britain, which had been quite good until the end of 2017, deteriorated gradually. Eighteen months of disappointing growth gave way, in mid-2019, to a deep recession the country was unable to pull itself out of. Zero percent interest rates were in place at the appointment of the new Governor of the Bank of England that same year, Mr Denniel, following the resignation of his predecessor. Although he kept them at that rate, it failed to stimulate an economy now paralysed by an absence of investment, businesses relocating, and a collapse in spending.

In 2021, five years after the Brexit vote, the value of the pound sterling was 40% lower than its historic lowest level, inflation was hitting the purchasing power of households, and unemployment was paralysing all regions of the country.

Admittedly, modern crises do not result in such ostentatiously grim effects as in the past, like the Great Depression of the 1930s. There were no long lines of the unemployed waiting for soup kitchens in the street. The wealth of the country was such, at the time of the vote, that the economic slowdown had only partially affected it. Social protection mechanisms came into play. A tourist on a brief visit to the UK would probably not have noticed anything, especially in central London. The shops were open, the restaurants were full. But people were living less well. Most people were having trouble making ends meet. And when you went to the suburbs, or to the provinces, you saw the shuttered factories and out of business shops. Imported goods were expensive; you had to economise on everything. Life in the United Kingdom at the end of 2021 was becoming difficult.

More seriously, the weakening of the economy led to fears of a major crisis in the event of further upheaval. The future was to prove that the country would not be spared this ordeal.

Dramatis personæ

(in alphabetical order of the surnames)

James Callagher, billionaire Chairman of the HGB Bank and of the Financial Club
Philip Denniel, Governor of the Bank of England
Jane Farrow, Philip Denniel's mother in law
Patrick Gills, Janet Gradens' husband
Janet Gradens, a young woman with mental health issues
Jeremy Jones, Leader of the Labour Party
John Klin, Economist
Edouard Marquet, French President
Tracy Meller, British Prime Minister
Nancy Mills, Nick Walderg's girlfriend
Laura Soriens, Chief Executive of HGB Bank
Luke Trosden, Market speculator
Mark Tweeds, Financial Analyst at Standards
Nick Walderg, Trader at HGB Bank
Guy Wick, leader of the Euro-sceptic movement in the Conservative Party

Thanks and acknowledgements

The information on Chequers comes mainly from the excellent book *Chequers, the Prime Minister's Country House and its History*, written by Norma Major, wife of former Prime Minister John Major. I express my gratitude to the author.

Details of the Black Country come in part from Wikipedia (https://en.wikipedia.org/wiki/Black_Country, available under the Creative Commons Attribution-ShareAlike License), and the March 2011 Dudley Borough Economic Assessment, published by the Dudley Metropolitan Borough Council. The information on the Chilterns comes from the beautiful website http://www.chilternsaonb.org. My thanks also to its authors.

Bloomberg's daily newsletter and The Times Brexit sections deserve special mention. Excellently put together and well referenced, they allow one to follow the twists and turns of a news story.

THANKS AND ACKNOWLEDGEMENTS

I am also grateful to Margaret Morrison, who translated the book from French to English. She did a fantastic job and provided me with precious advice.

Finally, I want to thank my wonderful wife Ghada for her proofreading and ongoing support. This book is dedicated to her as well as to our adorable daughter Maria.

CPSIA information can be obtained
at www.ICGtesting.com
Printed in the USA
LVHW041531060523
746309LV00002B/104